BLOOD

BLOOD

SARAH
PINBOROUGH

First published in Great Britain in 2024 by Gollancz
an imprint of The Orion Publishing Group Ltd
Carmelite House, 50 Victoria Embankment
London EC4Y 0DZ

An Hachette UK Company

The authorised representative in the EEA is Hachette Ireland,
8 Castlecourt Centre, Castleknock Road, Castleknock, Dublin 15,
D15 XTP3, Republic of Ireland (email: info@hbgi.ie)

1 3 5 7 9 10 8 6 4 2

A CIP catalogue record for this book is
available from the British Library.

ISBN (Paperback) 978 1 399 62345 2
ISBN (eBook) 978 1 399 62346 9

Typeset by Input Data Services Ltd, Bridgwater, Somerset

Printed in Great Britain by Clays Ltd, Elcograf S.p.A

MIX
Paper | Supporting
responsible forestry
FSC® C104740

www.gollancz.co.uk

These tales started with Gillian,
and they will finish with Gillian.
For you, Gillian, your boys,
Joe, Teddy and Tommy – and of course Chief.
Sometimes people really do live happily ever after ;-)

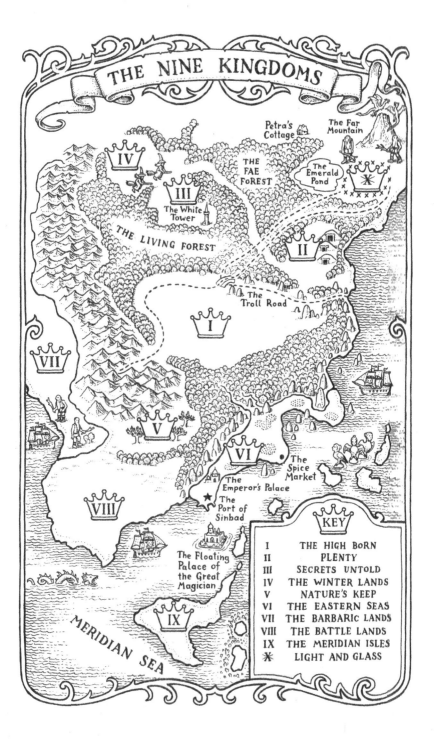

One

The new sigil on the flags hanging from the walls of the castle – a black rose entwined with an ice-white one – rippled in the breeze like true blooms. A rose for each queen, the pair of equal stature, and both now very much beloved by their people.

That last part still felt like a surprise to Lilith every time the crowds cheered her, but she also found she loved them back. Love was like that, it seemed. Once the spring was tapped, the amount of love a person had to give was endless.

Snow White had been gone all morning, breaking in a stallion, a beast as wild as Snow herself and as angry as Lilith's heart had once been, but a beautiful majestic creature nonetheless, a wedding gift from the storm-wracked Barbaric Lands. Snow had fallen in

1

love with the animal at once and had been eager to take him out for a ride as soon as he was settled into his new pasture.

Lilith had not worried about the horse bucking. Even if it did, Snow could manage the feistiest of mounts, and besides, all the animals in the kingdom loved her. She looked down from the window to see Snow returning, the horse subdued but happy beneath her, Snow's pale skin flushed with the excitement of the ride. So strange that it felt like only yesterday she had stood at this very window and looked down at Snow returning from a ride, her heart a maelstrom of envy and longing and bitterness. So much had changed since then. Not least that now Lilith always looked forward to what was to come in her marriage bed.

It was only just January, the new year feasts having left waists thicker and hearts more content, but the sun shone bright in the crisp air and all across the kingdoms an early spring was promised. Lilith looked down again and smiled, the breeze catching her pale hair so that it shimmered like silk as Snow waved up.

A dove had arrived while Snow was riding, bearing word that the young prince and his new wife, Rose, who all now believed to be Cinderella, had been delivered of a healthy baby girl, and despite everything that had happened between him and Snow White,

Lilith was happy for them. She had not behaved well herself during those dark times, and she knew what depths an unhappy heart could sink to. As it was, had it not been for the prince, she and Aurelia – although she would be forever Snow White – might never have admitted their love to one another.

She'd sent the bird back with their best wishes, reaffirming that if they needed anything, all they had to do was ask. The prince had found a good wife and perhaps she would turn him into a better man. Stranger things had happened.

But for now, Lilith put them from her mind. She and Snow had their own kingdom to manage, and it was a happy place now, the winter she had cast on it dispelled. She hadn't used her magic in the year since her wedding to Snow and, although she sometimes felt it fizzing inside her still, she was happy to let it lie dormant. Her magic sparked red not blue and she knew that wasn't right. *Unnatural* magic, those were the whispers she'd always heard and, despite questioning her great-grandmother incessantly, she'd never got an answer as to why that was. But she was happy, and happiness meant she had little call for magic. She'd locked up her room of magical items and sometimes even forgot they were there. She had no need of a hiding place anymore.

In the quiet morning air the songs of those heading to the foundries and mines carried to the castle. While most chose to continue in the work they'd been born into, dwarves were no longer limited to that occupation. Dreamy had started a theatre company that was proving a delight to the city, Stumpy helped balance the castle books, and Grouchy, who had cheered up now that the arthritis in his hands was being treated, had found a skill in ceramics and made wonderful dinner services that were very much in demand.

Yes, life in the kingdom was good.

She turned, her heart leaping as she heard footsteps coming up the stairs, two at a time.

'I knew you'd tame him,' she said, as Snow White flopped on their large bed, still panting from the ride. 'You always do.'

'No, I don't. I reach an understanding with them. It's different.' She grinned. 'Like I did with you.'

Lilith lay next to her wife, their faces close, and – as ever – she lost herself in Snow's violet eyes. She leaned forward and kissed her, the soft fullness of her lips and body never failing to excite her, and knowing, from the way she responded, that the same could be said for Snow. They were a perfect match, light and dark, fire and ice, and no one in the kingdom could any longer imagine it otherwise.

4

BLOOD

As she slipped out of her robe and pulled at the buttons of Snow's white riding shirt, her breath got heavier. 'There's a bath ready,' she whispered, breathless now, as their bodies entwined. 'Do you want it?'

'Later,' Snow whispered. 'I think I need to sweat some more first.'

And as her head dipped lower, her tongue tracing a line down Lilith's flat stomach, all thoughts of the prince and his family were forgotten. Lilith's breath came faster still as Snow traced her fingertips up Lilith's thigh, and her legs opened eagerly under their touch, exposing herself to Snow, wanting to feel the fingers slide inside her as Snow's tongue teased her. She would never tire of this, she thought as one hand teased her own nipple and she lost herself in the sensations that flooded her body. It had been a long road, but their adventures were over. From now on they were going to live happily and blissfully ever after.

Her fingers reached down, curling into Snow's glossy hair as her back arched and she became lost in the fire.

TWO

Time had lost all meaning for Rumpelstiltskin in the long century behind the hedge, but the year and more that had passed since he'd clawed his way through the bramble with the foolish prince and the huntsman had not eased his anger or loss. If anything, it had made it worse. He'd gone to Petra's grandmother as he'd been told to do – the huntsman and prince leaving him there – and while at first there had been tears of joy to meet his daughter's daughter, he'd discovered he felt no real connection to her.

She told him that after leaving the witch's tower, her mother, Rapunzel, had married a man twice her age and they had been very happy, but when he'd died, she'd left the village and come here to make her home in a clearing in the Fae Forest. She spent much of her time at the strange thicket wall, and when she returned to her child and her cottage, she would seem weighed down with something close to grief.

Rumpelstiltskin listened to her story and wondered why his daughter had never called out to him through the thicket as Petra had called to the wolf? Had she hated him for leaving her behind? Maybe she hadn't realised he was awake beyond the wall. Whichever was the truth, the woman Petra's grandmother described did not sound at all like the Rapunzel he had left behind. Settling down with an older man and living in a country village? That was not the life his daughter had dreamed of. She had loved her pretty dresses and handsome boys and lavish dances and glittering carriages. But then it had been so long, perhaps he no longer remembered her properly. That thought made his heart turn even more bitter.

When he left Petra's grandmother, they both knew that he wouldn't return and he thought that perhaps she, like him, had not felt the closeness that should be there when blood met blood. He followed the path he had taken with his daughter a hundred years before, past the Emerald Pond and out of the Fae Forest, all the way through the woods that shifted and changed around him as territories did, until he reached the Kingdom of Secrets Untold and found his way to the white tower, as if there had been breadcrumbs dropped to show him the route.

In the short years *before* he'd put Beauty to sleep, he'd never considered himself a violent man, but once he got to the tower and found it to be a ruin, he knew that his aim, subconscious as it had been, had been to kill the witch for what she'd taken from him. But that was not to be. It was over. The witch was long gone, and ivy and other climbing plants had made the crumbling stone their home.

He went inside and conquered the stairs, despite the gaps where some were missing and those that remained being slippery with moss. There were gaping holes in the walls that would be easy to fall from, but still he climbed, all the way up to the top. Birds flapped their wings at him, annoyed at their nests being disturbed, but Rumpelstiltskin left their raggedy homes alone and instead carefully looked through the dusty remnants of the witch's possessions.

Some books remained, warped with age, but many had vanished from the tilted shelves. Had they been stolen by passers-by or had the witch taken them herself? Why did she set Rapunzel free? Perhaps she had died and the tower had fallen into disrepair without magic to hold it together?

In the back of a rotting cupboard he found a small

half bottle of what looked like blood, which he pocketed, and then, up on the very highest floor, a room with a few old spinning wheels and spindles. He stared into it for a long moment before turning his back on them and heading back down to the forest. He had no truck with spindles anymore. He had been cursed by one as much as poor Beauty had. Better he had stayed alongside her and slept another hundred years. At least then he'd be oblivious to this pain.

The days merged into months as he drifted through the kingdoms, doing odd jobs here and there. He sharpened knives in the spice markets of the Eastern Seas, he weighed coal in the Winter Lands and although he liked the pain of the freezing temperatures, finding it a distraction from his guilt and loss, he left quickly after witnessing one of their notorious burnings. He found that while he wished death on the witch who'd stolen Rapunzel from him, he could not stomach the burning of others, and for weeks afterwards his dreams were haunted by the screams of agony that had come from the young woman who'd been dragged to the pyre, her fingers chopped off to stop her magic, as she died in the blaze. He walked and walked until her screams finally faded.

Everywhere he went, through all the forests of the kingdoms, memories of his child haunted him.

Rapunzel as a toddler running to him joyfully. Rapunzel and Beauty playing hide and seek before the Beast had made herself known. Rapunzel growing into a beautiful young woman, fascinated by dresses and balls, and worrying about her friend. The words on the note he left her burned behind his eyes as if branded into to his eyelids. *I love you with all my heart and I promise I'll come back for you soon. Papa.* He'd made a promise and broken it, and everyone knew a broken promise was the path to a curse. He had been cursed. His remaining life was a curse.

He walked through the winter, through the prince's kingdom, and found no peace for himself, and then he kept on, past the Troll Road and back into the forest. When his feet were too blistered from walking to continue, he set up a stall polishing leather shoes on the streets of Nature's Keep, a small kingdom of olive groves and fruit trees, dusty lanes and hot sun, close enough to the Battle Lands to know they never wanted war, where rain was rare but goats roamed free on arid land, and families ate well on figs and dried meats. In the evenings he would sit alone and drink wine and hope that the next day he would not wake at all. It was on one such evening there that he heard that the prince of the Kingdom of the High Born, the largest of the kingdoms and one of the wealthiest and most powerful, and his new wife, were expecting a child.

He did not touch a drop of wine after that, but packed his few possessions together, and left the heat and simple life behind, remembering the panicked promise of the weak prince.

I will give you my child. My first born.

He'd been so determined to break free from Beauty's grasp that he'd offered up an unborn infant in exchange for Beauty sleeping for another hundred years.

For the first time since the briar wall had grown around Rumpelstiltskin so long ago, a small flame of hope sprung up inside him. There might be a child to love. He deserved that baby, he decided, as his feet carried him through the days and nights of walking, pausing only to sleep and eat when exhaustion overcame him. The prince would not be alive without him, and so neither would that child.

He reached the Kingdom of the High Born just before the new year and took a small room in a coaching inn, washing pots to cover the cost. He paid his penny to go into the castle maze on a quiet afternoon and saw the prince's homely wife standing at a high window. Despite the distance between them he was sure their eyes met, just for a moment, and then the prince saw him too, and there was an expression of fear on the prince's face before his wife gasped, her eyes widening with surprise.

Rumpelstiltskin hurried away then, his heart leaping. The baby was coming. *His* baby was coming.

The next day, when the bells pealed out across the city and the kingdom, he laughed and cried with joy, and danced and drank in the square with the rest of the population. It truly was a wonderful day. A baby girl had been born.

His baby girl.

***

It was barely past ten in the morning, when Rose would normally be meeting the king and his ministers or reading *The Morning Post*, still warm and smelling of ink having come straight from her father's press. But today their little family was still at breakfast, Rose glowing with the first flush of motherhood as the prince refilled her teacup, before leaning over and planting a soft kiss on his daughter's head. He was as delighted as she in parenthood, as if he had grown up overnight, and once again Rose was surprised at the depth of love she had started to feel for him. It was mutual, she could see that. They had found what they needed, and discovered it was what they wanted.

True love was strange it seemed. And now they had little Giselle. Their lives were perfect. She was the luckiest woman in all the Nine Kingdoms.

'There's a man here to see you,' her husband's valet said, after politely knocking to disturb them. 'Something about a promise?' The young servant shuffled awkwardly. 'He won't leave. He's sitting on the floor in the reception room. Should I get the Royal Guard to remove him? Or talk to your father and—'

'Don't go to the king,' the prince cut in quickly. 'I can deal with this. Put him in the antechamber and I'll be through shortly.'

'As you wish, sire.'

Rose noted the prince's face had faded from tanned and healthy to ashen, and her stomach fluttered with unease. Suddenly she remembered the man in the dusty crimson jacket she'd seen in the maze. What was it the prince had said? He hadn't thought the man would find him. What else? There was something – before the waves of childbirth had distracted her.

I made a deal. And a deal is a deal.

She repeated the question she'd asked then, and found that she held baby Giselle tighter as she did so. 'What did you do?'

***

Rose was still reeling from the prince's admission when they'd donned their royal finery as if it were armour and gone to face Rumpelstiltskin. She'd left their daughter locked in the nursery, surrounded by guards, and let them think it was just a new mother's nervous disposition. She'd held her husband's trembling hand and they'd walked into the antechamber together to face the thin, grey-haired man in the dirty crimson jacket. He looked hungrily at Rose's empty arms and she knew that they were doomed, and he would not back down. She saw his grief, his loss, and the madness of a hundred years of sacrifice, and she couldn't even dislike him for it. She pitied him and feared what he could take from her, but she understood him.

Still, both she and the prince tried. They offered him rare black pearls stolen from poisonous oysters off the reefs near the Meridien Isles. Jewels from the Kingdom of Plenty. A lifetime of luxury. All these treasures Rumpelstiltskin refused with scorn.

'An orphaned infant, perhaps,' she said. 'There are many children in need of a loving home in the kingdom. Surely that would be better than—'

'I want what I was promised.' Rumpelstiltskin stood tall, the wrinkles deep in his thin face. 'And he promised me his first born.' He glanced at the pale and unhappy prince, full of poison. 'What kind of man gives away his child?'

'I didn't know,' the prince said. 'I didn't understand how much love I could feel. I've changed. I'm not the man you knew. *Please*, let me make this right with you. Why would you wish your own grief on someone else?'

'It was because of royal blood that I gave up my child, and it is a child of royal blood who will replace her. And how dare you equate the grief you will feel with what I have suffered. Your child will not be locked in a tower with a witch but will be loved and cared for more than you could have dreamed possible. You will have that comfort. I did not. And you cannot break your promise. A deal is a deal and a broken promise brings a curse.'

'Ten days,' Rose said suddenly. Time. That's what she needed. 'Give me ten days with my daughter.' She got up from her throne and went to stand close to Rumpelstiltskin so that he had to face her close up. 'My husband's foolishness has caused this situation. And while he may have been a young fool when he made you that vow, he is a noble man now, and will not break it. But none of this is my doing and it is also *my* loss.'

For a moment something flickered in the man's

eyes. Pity. Care, perhaps. He might be doing something monstrous, but he was not a monster, she was sure of it. And that gave her hope.

'My only regret is that you must suffer for a promise you did not make,' he said. 'I came immediately so that you would perhaps not feel so great a pain. But why the delay? To spend so long with your child will surely make giving her up more difficult?'

'I need to make my peace with it. To say my farewells.' She stood tall, not wanting to show her fear. 'And perhaps, when the time is up, if I can present an alternative solution to you that you find satisfactory, then you might release my husband from his obligation. This gives you ten days to consider changing your heart's desire too.'

There was a long pause before Rumpelstiltskin bowed his head. 'I will give you your time. But there is nothing that could be said to persuade me to change my mind, and nothing you can offer me of equal value. A royal child will be mine, madam. In ten days I will collect your daughter.'

And with that, he turned to leave.

As soon as he was gone, Rose's calm left her, and she paced frantically as the prince sat with his head in his hands.

'*Think*,' she said. 'There must be someone who can

reason with him. Persuade him against this course of action.'

'Perhaps the soldiers could ...' The handsome prince didn't finish the sentence, but she could see in his awful expression what he was suggesting.

'You think killing him will solve the problem? Promises make themselves heard, my love. I dread to think what calamity would befall us – or Giselle – were you to do that. No.' She paced some more and then paused at the window, looking down to where Rumpelstiltskin was walking away at a casual stroll as if he hadn't a care in the world. 'We need to find a way to make him release you from your vow.'

'I'm so sorry, Rose.' The prince got to his feet and came to hold his wife. 'If I could take it back I would in an instant. You know that I would do anything for you and Giselle. If he would take my life instead of our daughter I'd gladly give it.'

Heavy as her heart was, she knew his words to be true and found it hard to stay angry with him. He was a charming prince and he was *her* prince, and she'd known from the start that she would be the brains in the marriage and that he'd been unwise, to say the least, before their union.

'I'd even go back to that nightmare with the Beast

to save her.' He shuddered with the memory, but a thought struck Rose.

'Maybe that is where our answer lies,' she said. 'When you told me about your adventures, you said there was another trapped with Rumpelstiltskin for a hundred years. The wolf man. Is that right?'

'Yes. Toby. He stayed behind with Petra to use the spindle again and send Beauty and the kingdom back to sleep. Why?'

'They must have grown close over those hundred years. If anyone can persuade Rumpelstiltskin to release you from the vow, maybe he can?'

'You don't understand, Rose. He's behind the wall of briars which is now twice as thick as before. A second curse on the queen made it stronger. We barely got out alive.'

'It's worth a try, my love.'

'Then I shall go.' Despite the fear etched on his face, the prince held her tightly, and his arms were strong. He would go back there to save their child and she knew that he would not hesitate to do whatever it would take to protect them. He *had* changed.

'You are a good man,' she said, and kissed him gently. 'But you are not the man for this job.' She saw the hurt in his eyes and smiled. 'Not because you could not do it – I know you could – but you're needed here.

I need you. The kingdom needs you. And we cannot show that there is anything wrong. Your father cannot know of this predicament. You cannot leave.' She paused, holding his face in her hands. 'The huntsman. You must send the huntsman to fetch the wolf.'

Three

The huntsman had left the stallion the prince's men had given him behind as a surprise for Cinderella and taken his own mare on his reluctant journey through the forests. A reliable horse was better than a fast one, and the prince should have remembered that material gain had never had an influence on him. In fact, he'd nearly said no to the prince's request entirely, but could see that the young man was devastated and Rose was Cinderella's half-sister after all, and he knew Cinders still felt bad about Rose's toe and everything she'd gone through during the bride balls. If the huntsman had said no, Cinderella would go to try and save Rose's baby herself.

She'd probably do as well as he could, he thought, wryly. His wife excelled as a huntswoman and their greatest nights of passion were always after the competition of a hunt, sometimes both tracking an animal for two days or more before one of them took it down. She had been out on a hunt when the prince's messengers had arrived, and he hadn't waited for her to return before leaving. She was as wild as he now that she was truly herself and not dreaming of princes, and their love did not rely on asking the other's permission to do something. If he had waited she would have been angry with him for wasting the time, and as it was he would only be gone a few days.

They both enjoyed being apart – it made the reunions even more passionate. He was proud of what a strong member of the huntsman community Cinderella had become and he enjoyed seeing how she quietly impressed both the men and the women. He had found his true love, and he couldn't be happier. Perhaps for that, even without Rose being family, he would have gone on this last adventure for the prince. He would not have found Cinderella without having been the prince's babysitter through all his misadventures. And so here he was, returning to the briar wall.

It would be good to see Toby and Petra again if he could find a route through, he admitted to himself, and was surprised to feel a slight thrill at the adventure ahead. But first, he had to stop somewhere else he thought he'd never go again. There was no point going to a kingdom under a curse without a little assistance, and having seen how thick the briars had got when they left, it was going to be harder to get in this time. As he headed into the Kingdom of Plenty, he hoped that this time he wouldn't be leaving as a mouse.

***

Things had definitely changed, he thought, as he stood in the throne room at the top of the highest tower, light pouring in through the windows and shining on the two queens, one so pale with ice-white hair and the other rosy-cheeked and dark-haired, resplendently gorgeous and glowing and regal. Snow White was wearing riding breeches, now with ruby and diamond trim, while Lilith was in white, not black, her dress flowing more freely, no tight stays to bind her, her crown shining with diamonds that shot glittering rainbows through the sunlight dancing across the polished floor.

'This is an improvement on the black walls and red lightning décor,' he said, wryly. 'I take it you're both very happy?'

'Don't make me turn you into a mouse again,' Lilith replied as Snow White burst into laughter.

'I wish I'd seen that.'

'Don't tempt her,' the huntsman said. 'While it's certainly made me appreciate even the smallest of animals, I have no desire to return to that state. My wife wouldn't be pleased.'

'So we're not the only ones who are happy.' Lilith's face was not as thin as it had been at the height of her unhappiness, and he thought that under her dress, her body would be fuller too. He couldn't help but smile a little at the memory of his carnal time with both of them. Snow, out in the forest, and Lilith, right here on the floor, now knowing that they must both having been thinking of each other.

'I'm glad everything's worked out well. Your kingdom seems content too.' He'd seen the change in their sigil, the two roses entwined, and thought it very fitting.

'Our contentment is their contentment,' Lilith said with a smile, and the huntsman realised it was the first time he'd seen her look truly happy.

'I take it this isn't a social visit?' she finished, and the huntsman shook his head before explaining what he'd been tasked to do and telling them about Beauty and the Beast and Rumpelstiltskin and the cursed spindle.

'You won't be able to go in through the thicket,'

Lilith said when he'd finished. 'You're right. It's a double enchantment now – she's been twice cursed with the same magic – which will make the binding stronger. And also when you went last time, the hundred years was nearly up. This hasn't yet been two summers.'

'What about going under?' Snow asked, and they both looked at her. 'Could you tunnel under the thicket to get in?'

'It's very deep and I'm not sure how long that will take if time is of the essence? I'm a huntsman, I know nothing about how to make tunnels safe, or how best to dig through the earth. I can *try* but—'

'You won't have to,' Snow sprang to her feet. 'I know exactly who can help.'

She led the way, running down the stairs, and he and Lilith followed – it was a lot quicker as a man than as a mouse – until the sound of discordant music hit them, coming from behind a large, arched doorway, followed by a despairing cry of, *'No, no, no, it's step ball change on the left foot. The left!'*

With a grin, Snow White threw open the doors and clapped her hands. The huntsman was relieved that the cacophony coming from the brass band stopped immediately, replaced by a chorus of mumbled, 'Your Majesties'.

'Snow!' Dreamy exclaimed, happily. 'You shouldn't be here.' He looked past her to Lilith. 'And *you* definitely shouldn't be. This show is a surprise extravaganza for your birthday.'

'I can't wait,' Lilith said, dryly.

The huntsman had seen the hardy mining dwarves on his travels through the kingdom before, but none so flamboyantly dressed as Dreamy was, in satin breeches, an extravagant hat and a silk scarf draped casually around his neck.

'I'm sure it will be wonderful,' Snow said, giving the diminutive man a hug. 'But for now we need to speak to you privately. You and Grouchy and a couple of the others. I need you to do something for me.'

'Anything, Snow, you know that.'

He shooed his cast and musicians away and listened to what Snow and the huntsman were requesting.

'It might be fun to dig again,' he said when they'd finished. 'And in softer ground too. We can navigate any roots, I'm sure. They'll only go down so deep.' The huntsman watched as the dwarf's eyes narrowed, his mind already calculating the job.

'There is something else I should mention,' Lilith cut in. 'You're going into an enchanted kingdom. And there's a very good chance that you'll fall sound asleep as soon as you break the surface.'

The huntsman, the dwarf, and Snow White all stared at her. He raised an eyebrow. 'And there I was thinking this would be easy.'

'Like I said, the enchantment is stronger now. Only someone *already* enchanted is likely to be untouched by the curse.'

'Am I supposed to shout to Toby through the tunnel? What if he and Petra don't even see the tunnel, let alone hear me? What's the point of going there if I can't get in?' A thought struck him and his stomach sank. 'Don't tell me you're going to turn me into a mouse again.'

Lilith smiled, amused. 'Tempting as it is to use my magic on you again, sadly not. You can't cheat magic. But you will have to escort someone who *can* get in first. Someone already under a curse. And while I will use my power to ensure he can't hurt anyone while you do so, if anyone can find a way around a spell, it will be him.'

'Who?' Snow White asked.

'Someone I hoped never to have to speak to again.' She paused, momentarily pained. 'He gave me the comb that killed Tillie the serving maid. He promised me it brought happiness.'

'Some would say that death does bring happiness,' the huntsman said. 'It certainly brings peace.'

26

'That's how he riddled his words. But there was no peace in poor Tillie's face.' She was suddenly fraught with tension, almost as tense as she had been when they had first met. 'Trust me when I tell you that the boy is a monster. And you must bring him straight back here when the task is done. Do you understand?'

The huntsman nodded, and took heed, already looking forward to getting back to his life in the forest. The business of royals was never easy, he'd learned, nothing about this trip so far was changing his mind. 'You'd better fetch him then,' he said. 'The sooner I leave, the sooner you get him back. And one day of the ten is already gone.'

'Snow, why don't you and our guest have some lunch,' Lilith said. 'Dreamy, please fetch your friends, if they're willing to come, and ask cook to provide some provisions. This may me take a little while.'

Four

It was strange to be back in the small room that had been her refuge from her first marriage. They had revitalised the library beyond – the glass dome was clean once more, the wooden floor polished, and all members of the castle's household were encouraged to peruse the books that filled every inch of wall space – but the locked, secret, windowless room at the back had been untouched since her return with Snow White from the Kingdom of the High Born more than a year before.

She lit the candles to dispel the darkness that radiated from the black walls, but it was still gloomy. Everything was as she'd left it, wine in a carafe on the mahogany table now no doubt sour and grainy. Her glass cabinets, legs forged from dragon bone, shone clean, although she was sure that here and there dust would have found its way in, under the door perhaps, and soon this would be like a tomb, all forgotten, for someone perhaps a hundred years from now to find. Someone with new adventures to have. More curses and spells and magic and true love, as was the way of the Nine Kingdoms.

In the corner, the wooden door of the cabinet creaked open. *'Snow White is the fairest in all the lands.'*

'Yes. Yes, she is,' Lilith said with a smile, and pushed the door closed again, before unlocking one of the glass cabinets and reaching for an item at the top.

The small bronze lamp that she'd sealed up with gold.

Was she doing the right thing? She wasn't sure, but there was no other option. Magic couldn't be cheated – she couldn't curse someone just to get into Beauty's kingdom. And the only creature she knew who was currently under a spell was the man-child who had been tricked into becoming a genie. The one who had tried to kill her and very nearly killed her true love.

Aladdin.

She mixed various potions from her drawer of liquids and tinctures into a bowl, and then carefully, so as not to splash herself, dipped the lamp into it. As soon as the metal made contact a burst of hot steam rose into the air, the gold painted layer starting to dissolve, hints of tarnished bronze slowly showing through. She left the lamp there and considered how best to charm the boy inside and then, when the spout was free of gold, she pricked her finger and let two drops fall inside, before muttering her chosen charm and letting red sparks fly from her fingertips.

Witch's blood was not necessary for all magic, but for any charms or curses regarding death – either preventing it or causing it – it was always advised. That was what her great-grandmother had taught her and it was better to be safe than sorry.

She stood back and took a deep breath, stealing a moment before summoning the boy. It felt good to let her magic live again –tingling under her skin, almost sexual, a burst of bright energy inside her. Perhaps she could find a way to use it occasionally. She'd spent so many years denying who she was, one way or another, that now that she was happy in her personal life she needed to find an outlet for the gift she'd been so afraid of using when she'd been growing up in the Winter Lands.

Perhaps a school, she thought, thinking of the library on the other side of the door, and the vastness of the west wing that, in the main, remained unused. A haven for witches from all over the Nine Kingdoms. Perhaps that was something she could do. The thought made her fingernails glitter red and brought a smile to her lips, finally giving her the confidence to summon the boy.

She stood tall as she rubbed the bronze and battered lamp. The small figure rose from the spout, hidden in a whirlwind that threatened to take her off her feet, and then when it calmed, there he was in front of her.

'You summoned me, master.' She was surprised to see that the man-child, dressed in the same loose trousers and waistcoat of a genie, was now more man than child. His skin was still bright and earthy brown, and his eyes were still dark and clever, but there was a hint of stubble on his chin. Her surprise must have been visible for he continued, 'I think your rage after my last mishap, aged me a little.' She said nothing. Fifteen or eighteen he was still the same murderous street urchin from the Eastern Seas.

She had expected him to be filled with rage, and while she was sure that once he'd grown used to a little freedom he would start planning his revenge, all she could see in this moment was relief. He was no fan of small spaces, and he had spent a very long time trapped in the lamp before he had come into her possession – he had probably expected to be stuck inside forever this time.

No, she thought, as she told him what was required

of him, Aladdin was no match for her.

***

'Will they be all right?' Snow asked as they watched the odd group leave from the battlements of the castle. The dwarves were in a fine mood, always happy to do anything for their beloved Snow White, already singing as they marched, backpacks laden with dwarf ale, following the huntsman on his mare with Aladdin behind him.

'Time will tell. Aladdin can't hurt them, though. I've made sure of that.'

'They're off on an adventure,' Snow said wistfully, as they turned back inside to get on with the business of ruling.

There was something sad in her voice that made Lilith pause. 'I think we've have enough adventures, don't you?'

'I didn't have one,' Snow shrugged. 'Everyone else did, but I was asleep in a box the whole time. I guess I just – well, I would have liked to have known what it was like to do something important. Special.'

Lilith smiled and kissed her. She'd never thought of it that way. 'We're young,' she said, softly. 'There's still time.'

Five

It had taken Aladdin a day to adjust to the fresh air, and he was almost giddy from the overload to his senses. The colours, the light, the people, the noise, the *freedom* of it all. Being stuck in the lamp had been bad enough *before* Lilith had sealed the spout up with gold, but afterwards it was like he'd been buried alive. It had been so hot he was always thirsty, even though he had no need of food and drink when he was inside, the moist air laden with the tang of rusting bronze, only the solitary yellow candle on the wall for light, and the sand itching under him while he slept. He'd hated small places even before he'd spent days hidden under Rapunzel's bed, and as the weeks in the lamp merged into months, he'd felt suffocated and forgotten, even his rage giving way to a self-pitying madness where he went from screaming to crying to cursing Lilith aloud with all the ways he would take his revenge should he ever get free.

As it was, he was so relieved to be summoned, for the spout to be clear again, that he'd almost simpered with gratitude – another sin he was struggling to forgive himself for. Still, now he had time to contemplate his revenge. Lilith had promised that she would let him out once a year for two weeks as long as he went on this quest with the huntsman and did as she bade him, and while that seemed so very little, it was better than never being let out again. Of course he'd agreed to it. He'd also expected more anger from her, but she hadn't even mentioned the poisoned comb.

On reflection, he was glad she hadn't used the comb on herself. He might not have thought that particular plan through carefully enough. He became the genie when he killed the Great Magician for the lamp. What might happen to a genie who killed its master? Freedom or death? He made a note to find out, either on this trip or his next release. After that he could plan. He had no doubt that Lilith would keep to her word. She'd changed, he could see that. She was softer now, which came as a surprise. And in love, which made him lose his last ounce of respect for her. He preferred her bitterness and cruelty. He could understand that.

Love was for fools and he didn't understand it at all.

As their small procession travelled from the Living Forest to the Fae one, the leaves around them had turned to a lighter green and the air carried the scent of a hundred flowers, some only found here. If he'd been forced to, he could probably have isolated and named most of them – another surprise to him. It would certainly have surprised his dead father, who thought nothing he'd ever tried to teach Aladdin about the spices and perfume makers of the markets of the Eastern Seas had sunk in.

It was all decidedly pleasant, Aladdin concluded, as the mare sauntered along beneath him. The only thing that marred his good mood was his complete inability to cause anyone any harm. He'd tried three times to reach for the knife at the huntsman's waist and each time his hand had diverted to slap himself hard around his own face, an action which caused his travelling companions as much mirth as it did him annoyance, even the grumpiest of the little band of four dwarves beside him laughing in merriment.

'I would never let you at my back, young monster,' the huntsman had said with a smile, 'if you weren't enchanted to behave.'

A similar travesty had occurred when they'd paused at the Emerald Pond and Dreamy, excited and thinking he'd seen a water witch, had leaned too far over and nearly fallen. Aladdin's natural instinct – and, in fact, inclination, because there were only so many renditions of Dreamy's songs from the birthday show he was planning called 'The Ice Queen Who Melted' he could take – was to push the small man in. It was certainly his *intention*, up until the second he found himself leaping forward to pull him back to safety instead.

Dreamy couldn't stop thanking him for saving his life, despite Aladdin's protests that he'd been aiming for the opposite, and it was then he realised how strong Lilith's binding magic really was.

He could only attack someone in order to save his companions or himself and, even then, only to injure and not to end life. Coming from the woman who had once asked for her current wife's heart – as the stories the dwarves couldn't help tell as they walked implied – this seemed entirely unfair. He'd happily kill the huntsman if he could, simply for being so handsome and at ease and ready to take on any quest.

Heroes. The world could live without them. *Should* live without them.

Still, he thought, as they paused to rest in a clearing, smoke rising up from the chimney of a cottage nearby, he was free, even if he wore invisible shackles.

He could eat and drink and explore. And maybe, when he reached the sleeping Kingdom of Light and Glass, he'd find a way to free himself from Lilith and her infernal lamp.

'There's someone we need to say hello to before we start digging.' The huntsman glanced behind him and waited for Aladdin to scramble from the mare before casually swinging his leg over and dropping down. 'And to let her know she might be getting a welcome visit from family.'

Six

The cottage was warm, a fire roaring in the grate. The huntsman almost laughed aloud when the four dwarves and the genie recoiled in horror from the grey-furred wolf with the sharp teeth and black eyes sitting in the rocking chair beside it, busy knitting a scarf. Only then did the old lady straighten up, revealing her face beneath the dead wolf's head.

'I'm glad you're still using that,' the huntsman said, kissing her on the cheek and ignoring Aladdin's expletives. He'd tried to attack the 'wolf', with a knife grabbed from her bowl, and ended up slapping himself in the face again.

'You were right,' the old woman said. 'It keeps the winter wolves away. And it's ever so warm and comfy. How good to see you again, you handsome man.

But why are you back here? I've tried to call for Petra but the thicket is so high and full we can't hear each other.'

She smiled, but he could see the hurt in her eyes at her separation from her grandchild. She had been right to let Petra go, but it didn't make her loss any lighter, and he hoped he wasn't offering something he wouldn't be able to deliver.

'If our plan goes well then maybe you'll be able to talk to her again.'

'Oh, that would be wonderful, but first you must tell me about this quest,' she said, as she bustled to the kitchen. 'I have some stew here. You must all eat. Especially you, young man.' She beamed at Aladdin. 'You look like you could use a good meal. Need to fill out for when the girls come calling.' Aladdin smiled charmingly and started to help fetching the bowls and spoons, chatting away. The huntsman could see Petra's grandmother falling under his spell, and was reminded that though she was an old lady in a wolf's skin, she was far too sweet to recognise a wolf in sheep's clothing.

They ate and talked, sharing their latest tales – she of the visit from Rumpelstiltskin, he of the continued adventures with the prince and then Cinderella and finally back to Rumpelstiltskin and his new demands.

She listened, rapt, and it was clear that while she might be content, she did miss company.

'That wood store needs some repairs,' Grouchy said gruffly when he and Feisty came back in with some more logs for her fire. 'I'll mend that for you, once our digging is done. And I'll sort that bit of thatch that needs doing by the chimney.' He turned away to put the logs in the basket. 'Couldn't help but notice.' His face was lowered but the huntsman was sure he saw a flush of pink at the dwarf's collar.

'That would be very kind of you,' Petra's grand-mother answered, and patted at her silver hair. 'And I would be glad of the company.'

If Grouchy had gone a little pink before, he turned bright red at that. Well, well, the huntsman thought with a wry smile. Maybe she wouldn't be lonely for much longer, after all.

Once they'd eaten their fill and regained their energy, they took some bread and cheese that Petra's grandmother insisted on giving them, and headed to the wall of greenery.

No one spoke when they got there, all straining their necks to try to see the top of the briars. The hedge was far higher than the huntsman remembered, and thicker too, and the air was cooler around them, the grass thinner after constantly being in its shadow.

He stared at it, and the branches and leaves pulsed slightly as if perhaps they were alive.

'Well, climbing over isn't an option,' Aladdin said. 'I'm good, but I'm not risking falling from up there.'

'That would be the least of your problems, trust me,' the huntsman said, remembering how the briars and vines and branches had tried to ensnare him the last time he'd fought his way through. They'd probably tangle him into their heart and suffocate the boy if he tried to climb over.

The four dwarves – Grouchy, Feisty, Bolshy and Dreamy – unpacked their tools from their knapsacks – picks, spades, shovels and various other items that the huntsman was sure Aladdin was eyeing as possible instruments of torture – and murmured to each other, Feisty pressing the mossy earth, while Dreamy studied the bottom of the hedge, and Grouchy and Bolshy talked together. Soon a plan was agreed.

'The roots are going to be a problem. But we'll do our best to go around them or prop them out of the way,' Bolshy said. 'You agree, Grouchy? If you can remember how digging works now that you're in the crockery trade?'

'I was digging mines before you could hold a pick,' Grouchy growled, but the banter was all in good humour. 'And even Stumpy could dig better than you – and I mean *after* he lost his hand.'

He lifted his spade and drove it deep into the soft earth. As the others seamlessly fell into work beside him, Feisty started to hum, and within a minute, all four were singing quietly in harmony as they worked.

The huntsman began setting up camp a little further back from the thicket, and while Aladdin fetched kindling and wood from the edge of the forest, he went in search of something heartier for their dinner. Perhaps it was the proximity of the cursed kingdom but the wildlife was slower here and within a short time, and with very little satisfaction from the hunt, he returned with three rabbits and a fish from the river. He crouched by the fire to prepare them.

'I could skin those for you,' Aladdin said, adding some twigs to the growing flames. 'And gut them. I'm good with a knife.'

'I believe it.' There was a hunger in the boy's eyes that was beyond predatory. 'The queen told me some stories of you before she let you out.'

'I am what I am.' Aladdin shrugged. 'I can't fight my nature.'

'Probably how you ended up in the lamp.'

'No.' Aladdin smiled, his dark eyes suddenly full

of self-aware humour. 'My very ordinary greed let me down. I should have stuck with murder.'

'Huntsman!' Dreamy's shout reached them just as the huntsman found himself laughing with the boy. 'We have a problem.'

He got to his feet to go and paused before tossing Aladdin the knife. 'Don't wreck the skins. They'll make good boots for winter.'

Aladdin caught the blade expertly and grinned, looking happy for the first time since they'd left the castle. Despite everything he knew Aladdin had done – and that he had likely done much worse he didn't know about – the huntsman didn't dislike the genie. He was, as he'd said, as nature had made him, and you couldn't hate a person for that. He was amusing and smart and in some ways a far better travelling companion than the foolish young prince had ever been.

As he hurried over to where Feisty lay panting heavily on the ground, the huntsman realised that he and Aladdin had one thing in common. If it wasn't for Lilith's powerful magic keeping Aladdin in check, they'd both slit the other's throat at the first opportunity. Aladdin because killing was what he did, and the huntsman because that's what you did when there was a fox in a chicken coop.

'Is he all right?'

Feisty was pale and yawning, but waved away the water Grouchy offered, and was getting to his feet by the time the huntsman had reached them.

'I'm fine. I'm fine. I just suddenly felt very tired as I moved those root tips and blocked them behind some wood.' He shook out his limbs. 'I'm all right now. Just needed some fresh air.'

They'd been working for two hours, digging down deep before even trying to go forward, and all four dwarves were covered in dirt and looked more exhausted than hardy mine workers should. This was soft earth, not rock. Something else was doing this to them.

'The enchantment,' the huntsman muttered, peering into the narrow tunnel. They'd got quite far, and he could make out the flicker of a lamp deep underground, a lonely yellow glow creating shadows of movement like mice in the dark. 'As you're crossing the border it's starting to work on you.'

'Did this happen last time?' Dreamy asked, and the huntsman shook his head.

'Stronger magic this time.'

'We'll need a rope,' Bolshy said, sticking his spade in the ground. 'And to keep our distance from each other while passing the earth back. Then when whoever's at the front falls asleep we can pull them back and we'll know that's as far as we can go.'

'Makes sense,' the huntsman nodded. 'Someone needs to go back to Petra's grandmother's and ask her for some—'

'I'll go,' Grouchy cut in, almost too quickly. 'I saw some rope in her outhouse.'

'Off you go then,' the huntsman grinned, the dwarves smiling beside him. He wasn't the only one who'd noticed Grouchy's blushes in the cottage then. 'Maybe when you've brought the rope you can go back and get on with the chores she needs doing. If only one of you can dig at a time, there's no point in all four of you being here.'

'If you think that's a good idea,' Grouchy said, his voice gruff in a pretence of reluctance, already turning to leave. 'I suppose someone should.'

'How are we going to get to the other side if we fall asleep in there?' Dreamy asked. 'We tried shouting but we were too far down for anyone to hear us, even if they were close to the hedge, so they can't dig through from their side.'

'Even if they could, what do they know of shoring up the walls? Making a tunnel safe?' Feisty added. 'The whole thing could cave in.'

'Maybe keep that to yourself,' the huntsman said

dryly. 'There's only one person who can get through, and while he doesn't give other people's lives much thought, I don't think he's too keen on risking his own.'

Seven

'The whole thing could cave in.' Aladdin was aghast. He'd thought he would just dart through the tunnel when it was finished, in and out so quickly he didn't have to think about being under all that earth as if he was dead. Death was something he did to other people. He didn't care for it being applied to himself. 'I'd be trapped. Buried alive.' He'd had enough of feeling trapped in the lamp, he hadn't got out only to be suffocated under all that earth.

'You'll have a rope around you,' Dreamy said. 'If something goes wrong, we'll pull you out.'

'If we can,' Bolshy added. 'Depending on how much earth comes down. You might be—'

'You're not helping,' the huntsman said, winking at the dwarf. 'A little optimism goes a long way. Besides,

I trust your work. And it's not that much further is it? A few feet upwards and the earth has been loosened by all the digging already. It shouldn't take you long to get through, Aladdin. And I get the feeling that you have the luck of nine cats with nine lives each.'

'I was turned into a genie,' Aladdin said. 'How is that lucky?' He stared down into the hole and the flickering lamp beyond. At least it wasn't pitch black in there. That was something. 'But I suppose if I don't want to go straight back into the lamp then I have no choice?'

'You would suppose right.' The huntsman grinned. 'I knew you were clever.'

'Then I may as well start.' Aladdin took a pick and shovel from Feisty and tucked a gourd of water into his waist band.

'Get to the other side and shout out for Petra and Toby. They'll hear you. If they don't, then go further into the city and shout some more.'

'Just shout?'

'You'll be the only three living creatures awake. Trust me, they'll hear you. Tell Toby to come back with you. We need his help.'

'You've told me this three times already.' Aladdin dropped into the hole, the air immediately cooler surrounded by the earth. 'It's hardly a complicated instruction.'

'And whatever you do, don't go into the castle. Don't go *near* the castle.'

'What if they're *in* the castle?' Aladdin looked up, curious. 'And what's wrong with the castle?'

'Wait till they come outside.' He crouched by Aladdin. 'And don't worry about what's wrong with the castle. Just don't go there.'

'Why won't you tell me?' Aladdin asked, and the huntsman's handsome face crinkled into a tanned smile.

'Because, my young travelling companion,' the huntsman said, squeezing his shoulder, 'I understand you. Most people are dangerous without knowledge. I suspect you, on the other hand, are more dangerous *with* it.'

Aladdin couldn't help but grin back. 'Perhaps you're cleverer than I thought too.' He checked the rope knot was secure around him and then crouched and crawled down through the tunnel, deep into the earth. It stank of moisture and growth and goodness and, keeping his focus on the thin yellow light from the small lantern that was getting closer, Aladdin pushed forward until the tunnel started to curve upwards. When he reached the dead end, he started to dig.

He'd been digging upwards for about an hour, sweating hard, dirt covering him from head to toe and making his eyes sting, when he felt something brushing across his back. He turned as best he could in the cramped space to see what looked like a mass of worms wriggling through from the earth above, and others snaking round the narrow boards that propped the walls up further back. Another clump appeared, tendrils reaching down, like hungry, grasping fingers, reaching for something to dig into, almost quivering when they touched the cold earth under Aladdin. He realised what they were just as one of the dwarves behind him shouted, 'Roots! The roots are growing to block the tunnel! Hurry!'

Not needing to be told twice, all sense of method left him, and, muttering the foulest curses ever spoken by even the worst pirates from the seas beyond the Barbaric Lands, he scooped out big shovelfuls of earth, not caring that the dirt was coming down on him like a shower. He dug and dug until finally a small hole of sunlight appeared, just like the light did in the spout of the lamp, and warm, fresh air assailed him.

He scrambled upwards, but something yanked him back, and, in horror, he realised the roots had wrapped round the rope that was attached to his waist, dragging him down into the dark. As his feet slid backwards he tugged at the knots he'd been keen to make sure were tight on the way into the tunnel, and turned his muttered curses inwards towards himself. He was not going to get snared by the roots. He'd had quite enough of being trapped for one lifetime and he was not going to let it happen here, not doing something good for someone else. His nimble fingers worked faster and just as he got the knot undone the rope was sucked back down into the dirt. Aladdin climbed, agile and eager, until he wriggled free of the earth and slumped, panting, onto the warm soft ground, sweating and laughing up at the sun. He was free. At least for a little while.

'I made it,' he called back down the tunnel, but no answer came and after trying again, he got to his feet and stared out at the waiting kingdom. There was a strange, complete silence in the air, almost eerie, not even a breeze to rustle the leaves and thistles growing behind him or the branches of the trees here and there around him, no birds singing or flies buzzing.

Nothing.

He strode forward, his footsteps loud. 'Toby? Petra?' he called out. The huntsman was right. His voice, the only noise in the whole kingdom, as far as he could tell, was like a tolling bell, surely audible for at least a mile or more. He called again, walking

51

further along the hedge towards where two soldiers lay unmoving on the ground. While he found most people entertaining but disposable at best, and dull and immediately discardable at worst, soldiers he was happy to despatch without any hesitation and avoid where possible. He was happy to see – as the huntsman had told him to expect – that these two were fast asleep.

In front of them, one arm hung out of the thicket but the plants were so dense it might as well have been severed for how much Aladdin could see of the owner. At least he was asleep too and knew nothing of his entrapment. It would have been very different for Aladdin had he been caught in the roots. Once again, as he took a knife from the belt of one of the soldiers and tucked it into his waistband, resisting the urge to kick the man because it would only result in his slapping his own face, he wondered how someone as clever as he had found himself enslaved into doing the bidding of others. One day, the world would be his oyster. His plaything to do with as he pleased. And pleasing him, after all of this, was probably going to involve a lot of blood and none of it his.

He called out once more for Toby and Petra and again there was no answer, and so, with no other choice, he started walking towards the city, calling their names every fifty paces or so. He was quite pleased they didn't answer. It gave him some time to himself while still doing what he was bound to. There had been no point in running away – he'd learned that the first time Queen Lilith had let him out of the lamp – she could summon him back with a click of her fingers. Whatever freedom he had was temporary, and granted entirely on her whim. She had never made a wish beyond that first one to control his coming and going from the lamp – so there was no point in fighting it until he knew how to free himself from her magic. *Lucky*, he thought as he walked from the grassy path onto a clean street, thinking about what the huntsman had said. If he'd had any luck at all, his lamp would have been found by a stupid-yet-greedy fool and he'd have been out by now.

Still, here he was, alone at last, on a blissfully quiet morning in a strange kingdom. It was hard to stay in a foul mood with such an adventure in front of him and the Far Mountain large on the horizon, the source of all the life and energy in the kingdoms, protected by its walls of ice and home to the dragon's cauldron at its centre. On a clear day, regardless of where in the kingdoms you were, the cloudy peak of the Far Mountain could always be seen, but Aladdin had never been so close before and perhaps it was that proximity that put a spring in his step despite his century and more of woes.

As he walked, occasionally calling out and still getting no answer, he headed further into the heart of what was clearly a bustling, prosperous kingdom. It was something to behold, compared to the markets and dust of the Eastern Seas. He never seen so many windows, clean and clear in buildings of pale stone. Even the poorest houses had glass, something that was rare in Sinbad outside of the emperor's palace and the richest merchants' homes. Most ordinary people made do with wooden shutters, and he wondered what it must be like to live in a home with so much sunlight.

Everything was clean, and there were only a few people asleep in the roads and pathways, and most of them were soldiers or street cleaners, and so he presumed that the curse must have befallen them in the night. A curious look through one or two houses confirmed his suspicions. The residents were asleep in their beds or in chairs by firesides, a book tumbled to the floor beside them, fires continuing to burn as if just lit.

In one more opulent house, after climbing in through an unlocked window, he took a careful sip from a glass of wine and found it still perfectly fine, and deliciously heady, and so he took some more, and some bread and cheese, to eat as he explored.

In each of the market squares bunting was clearly going up, and there were little stalls mid-set up too, ready perhaps for food and drink to be sold. The bunting was silver and gold, the colours suiting the buildings, and looking at one of the crests he saw that this was the Kingdom of Light and Glass. What were they celebrating, he wondered, as elsewhere chains of flowers decorated the doorways. A noble wedding, or maybe even a royal one?

He looked up at the castle at the heart of the city, built with so much glass it glittered like a diamond. With the Far Mountain as a backdrop, it was breath-takingly beautiful, even for someone like Aladdin, who found it hard to rouse emotion for anything.

Whichever path he took led closer to it, but he still got no answer to his calls, and shouting was starting to make his throat hurt. Where could they be? Maybe they'd fallen asleep too somewhere? He was craving something sweet – perhaps a pastry and some cool water and maybe another glass of wine to wash it all down, but everything was locked up, and his eyes kept returning to the castle. The kitchens there would have the finest cakes, he was sure, and it wasn't Lilith who'd told him not to go there, it was the huntsman, so no magic could stop him.

The castle. That's where he'd go. Just to the kitchens. It wasn't *his* fault that Petra and Toby couldn't be found.

Guilt-free – which, to be fair, was how he did everything in his life – Aladdin headed towards the castle.

Eight

'You and Rumpelstiltskin lived here alone for one hundred years.' Petra, amused, made a chalk mark on the wall as they reached another crossroads. 'And you never found these tunnels. *I* found them in less than two years.' She smiled, mischievously, at Toby, who leaned against the wall beside her, holding the torch to light their way, his green eyes watching her, the yellow flecks in them startlingly bright in the flame's glow. 'And I thought that nose of yours could smell these things out?'

'Speaking of noses, it turns out you're a *lot* nosier about other people's houses than I ever was.'

'And if I wasn't we wouldn't eat from such fine crockery and sleep on such fine linen.' She leaned in and kissed him. 'And we wouldn't have found that trapdoor. And so here we are. On a little adventure.'

His stubble, always there regardless of whether he shaved or not, felt good against her soft face, and, as her stomach tingled with the tease of his tongue against hers, she was once again reminded of how lucky they were to be here together. Most couples might have twenty years together. They would have another ninety-eight without getting any older or changing in any way. Ninety-eight years to love each other in peace. Her only sadness was knowing she'd never see her grandmother again. She'd tried calling to her but the charmed hedge was twice as thick and twice as high as it had been before, and neither side could hear the other. But she could never have left Toby behind. He was her true love, and the days and nights sped by in passion and happiness, and, on the nights of the full moon, she would watch him race through the city, howling, and she would stand outside and howl back, as they used to in the time before they'd met.

'Concentrate,' he said, his strong hands around her waist doing little to make that instruction any easier, and she laughed, pushing him away so she could mark out the new paths on the tunnel map they'd started. It was fun to be doing this together. Often, they would take themselves to different parts of the city for the day, to paint or cook or draw or whatever took their fancy, and then come together in the evening to eat and talk. But this – her discovery of the tunnels – had given them both something interesting to do.

'That way's another dead end,' Toby said, concentrating as he sniffed at the air. 'I can smell wet bricks.'

Petra duly noted it down and then they carried on. These were secret thieves' tunnels, they'd figured that out quickly enough, and in the rabbit warren of paths that had probably been there for hundreds of years, there were a lot of dead ends, no doubt to confuse any soldiers if they chased the smugglers down here. It was an impressive network, secret doors coming up in various houses around the city and all leading to the castle. There was a secret doorway in a stable floor, one in the kitchen and another in a fireplace – all within the castle gates so things could be stolen without the soldiers on guard finding them.

It seemed that while most of the ministers had been preoccupied with trying to control the Beast, the minister for trade – a thin, tall man currently fast asleep in bed with a woman who clearly wasn't his wife – must have been busy lining his own pockets quite substantially from trading items that weren't his to sell.

Petra had found the first stash of silver in a baker's house – cutlery and a plate with the royal crest stamped on it – hidden in an unused oven when she'd been attempting to make croissants. She'd replaced it all in the castle and they'd made a vow not to buy their bread from that shop when the sleeping century had passed, but after that discovery she'd become curious, and it wasn't long before she'd found the trap door in the cellar. The thieves had taken linens and silks, clothes and jewels, as well as silver. All manner of expensive items that would fetch a pretty sum once out of the city.

'There,' she said, pointing ahead. 'Look. That must lead out of the city.' Toby held the torch up and she pointed to where a tunnel had been blocked off – not intentionally by the thieves but by thick roots that filled every inch of the space.

'The thicket wall,' Toby said. 'I wonder if anyone's trapped in there?'

'We'll find out in ninety-eight years, I guess.'

'I suppose so.' As he turned the torch back around, he paused. 'Is that a door?' Petra stared at the bricks and at first she couldn't see it but then, as Toby ran his hand over the surface, she saw the line – hidden but there. It *was* a door. 'I can smell something behind it. Smoked meats. Bread. Wine.'

They both studied the wall, touching the bricks, until one suddenly shifted under her touch and she smiled at Toby. 'That's it.' The door swung open to reveal a room set up to hide in – a large bed with clean, crisp sheets on it, water, wine, books, an area to use as a bathroom, lamps on the wall, and boxes of dried stores and bottles of water.

'Someone could hide here for a week,' Petra said, looking around her. 'Until soldiers stopped looking for you anyway.'

'Or stay for an hour,' Toby countered, pulling her to him. 'And mess up that perfectly made bed.'

Their faces were close, her strawberry blonde hair falling over one eye as his strong arms wrapped around her, but she pulled her mouth away from his, teasing. And teasing was all it was. They both knew how this game ended. The way it always did, with them both naked and sweating and temporarily satisfied.

'Shouldn't we go back up into the fresh air for that?'

'I think we should fuck like thieves,' he said softly, his words almost a growl as his mouth went to her neck, his hot tongue teasing down to her breasts. 'Right here.'

'As if soldiers were coming after us,' she breathed back, her heart thumping hard as her whole body tingled with his touch. 'And this was going to be the last time we'd have together for a while.'

'Maybe for ever.' He tugged at her dress until the

laces fell apart, and her skin was free. 'Maybe the gallows are waiting for us.'

He hitched her up and she wrapped her legs around his waist, eager for him to feel the wetness there as they kissed, lost in the fantasy, lost in each other, before he fell back on the bed. Flinging the last of her clothes to one side, she tugged at his breeches as his fingers slid between her legs, hearing him moan as he touched the delicate parts of her, and then, just as she could bear the longing no more, she guided him deep inside. It was her turn to moan and shudder as she rode him as a queen would a stallion, until she collapsed over him, pleasure engulfing her. He flipped her onto her back, and kissed her, moving slowly inside her until the heat came for her again, and then they were just Petra and Toby, not thieves on the run, and they whispered their love to each other until she felt his whole body stiffen over her and she relished his gasp as he came.

Nine

The closer Aladdin got to the castle the more people he found out on the streets having been caught mid-activity by the curse. Some were slumped on their carts, sleeping horses still on their feet, and others had crumpled by baskets of tumbled washing or bread or other goods that came and went at a castle when the nobility slept, and if there had been decorations going up around the city, they were nothing compared to the display at the castle. Flags and lights and huge flower garlands were mid-placement in the central courtyard just before the main entrance. Whoever was getting married, it was definitely a royal wedding.

As Aladdin stepped into the shadow of the enormous, beautiful building – an edifice to truly put the Great Magician's floating palace into perspective – he found two boys asleep on a pile of vines that they'd been cutting free from the pale front of the building.

All Aladdin knew about the curse that gripped the kingdom was that it had sent everyone who lived there, except the missing Petra and Toby, to sleep for a hundred years, and that the prince had woken them, and then promptly sent them back to sleep again. By the time these boys woke up again, the prince and the dwarves and Snow White and maybe even Lilith – although she had witch's blood and everyone knew witches could live a long, long life – would all be dead.

Maybe he would be too, if he could escape the genie curse. He'd been in the lamp a full year without release and now the fact he was out among people and *still* wasn't able to kill anyone was making him think about murder a lot. But he *was* allowed to kill anyone who threatened his life, so maybe, since the huntsman was so keen he stayed away from the castle, he'd find someone like that here. That would be fun.

He ignored the main steps up to the vast, glittering glass and heavy, wooden main doors and, with his belly and tastebuds still greedy for food, instead went round to where the tradesmen's entrances and the kitchens would be.

He was not disappointed. Every surface of the kitchen was filled with food of all varieties, ready for a feast to come and the breakfast and lunch before that and his eyes grew wide at the sight of a tray of pastries so large they could each fill a side plate. He took one and, after biting into the buttery deliciousness that almost melted in his mouth, pocketed two more before he moved on. In the vast pantry area a seven-tiered wedding cake was sectioned off and guarded by a sleeping chef. Aladdin cut himself a large slice, ate half of it, and then put the rest in the chef's hand and smeared some of the soft fondant icing around his mouth. Smiling, he went on his way.

He called out a few times as he explored the ground floor of the castle but still got no answer. The rooms were endless and the opulence grew tedious after a while, one beautiful room very much like all the rest, and the few doors that he found locked he couldn't be bothered trying to break into.

He did pocket a ruby and gold necklace, stolen from around a sleeping old noble woman's neck, and slipped the matching earrings in her dressing maid's pocket. He might not be able to do any physical harm, but there were still ways to cause trouble. With a growing sense of satisfaction, he committed a few more acts of such trickery before taking a bottle of wine from the huge array ready for serving in the ballroom, and headed up the sweeping central staircase.

Whose castle was this? Some over-indulged king no doubt. All kings and emperors grew fat. Perhaps one day he would too, all the cakes and pastries he enjoyed turning him smug and corpulent. Not yet though, he thought, as he ran up the stairs, enjoying feeling his lithe muscles work after so long imprisoned. But maybe one day when he was rich and powerful and had his revenge on all his enemies – starting with Lilith – he'd be so fat he'd have to be carried on a chair.

He made his way through various chambers, emptying piss pots on sleeping couples and switching underwear out of one room and into another, until finally he came to the most ornate jewel-encrusted doors.

There were two guards sleeping outside with feathers in their helmets and brighter uniforms than the others and, as he opened the door into the royal bedchamber, he found he'd quite forgotten the huntsman's words about avoiding the castle. Perhaps it was the wine he was drinking but, in fact, for the moment, he'd quite forgotten the huntsman existed at all.

***

The fire crackling in the grate had made the room exceptionally warm, and the blood in a small pool by the bed had thickened and congealed, the only thing he'd seen so far in this kingdom that had been touched by time or elements. He could see where it was coming from. The young queen – or so he presumed she was – lay sleeping in her bed, one arm hanging over the side, and he could see where the tiny drops of blood had fallen from the tip of her finger. Another was slowly, slowly forming there, so slowly it might take a week before it dropped to join the rest.

He looked at the girl, cloyingly sweet and perfect in a way that instantly irritated him, and then looked over to the other sleeping figure in the room. An old man, dressed in fine nobleman's clothes, a minister perhaps, was slumped in an armchair by the door. There was something on his lap, although he wasn't holding it, and Aladdin stared for a long moment before going and picking it up.

If anyone, up until now, had asked him if he believed in fate, he would have laughed scornfully and said that you make your own fate, but as he picked the spindle up and stared at it and then back at the girl in the bed, he suddenly wasn't so sure.

The spindle had a very sharp tip. He'd seen – he'd *stolen* – spindles like this from a white tower far away from here. Spindles charmed and cursed by a witch. He looked at the sleeping young woman's strange hair.

So shiny and dark but with thick strands of blonde on either side of her face. Hadn't Rapunzel talked about a girl like that? A best friend she half-remembered from her life before? Was *this* that girl? Had this been Rapunzel's home kingdom? Was this sleeping curse why her father had never returned to her?

He looked once again to the queen's bleeding finger, and whether it was the magic Lilith had placed on him to stop him hurting anyone or his own curiosity, he wasn't sure, but he felt an overwhelming urge to stop the bleeding. With the soldier's knife, he cut a strip from one of the expensive, perfectly white sheets and then carefully wrapped it around her pale, slim finger.

In an instant, he felt everything change. The fire in the grate crackled loud, immediately brighter, the noise almost making him jump after so much silence. The woman in the bed murmured, her eyes hazily starting to open.

'What have you done?'

Aladdin turned as the old man's eyes widened, horrified, taking in the scene he was waking to, until suddenly he leapt to his feet.

'I am the First Minister of this kingdom. Give me back that spindle. Quickly!' He rushed towards Aladdin, who darted backwards and sideways out of his reach. 'Prick her finger again!' the old man begged. 'This has to end! She *has* to die!'

Perhaps if he hadn't spoken the last sentence then all would have been well and Aladdin would have done as the First Minister said and everything would have returned to sleeping silence, but the magic Aladdin was under meant that instead of handing over the spindle to commit a hundred-year murder against the sleeping queen, he found himself throwing it into the blazing fire, where it instantly burst into strong, white, magical flames.

'No, you *fool!*' The minister lunged forwards, trying to reach into the fire and pull it out, but Aladdin pushed him backwards.

'What's happening?' the woman in the bed murmured, half-sitting up as the First Minister backed away. She looked around, bleary. 'Is it morning?'

'Why would you do that?' the old man groaned, ignoring her. 'After everything.' Tears sprang from his rheumy eyes. 'She has to die. This was the only way.'

He spun around, rushing out of the room, and the next thing Aladdin heard as the noises of the castle coming back to life grew to a cacophony was the heavy turning of a key in the lock.

Ten

Petra had just traced her mouth down the line of coarse hair from Toby's navel when the earth around them rumbled. She paused, looking up, her strawberry blonde hair messy from sex tumbling around her face, and her hazy expression becoming more alert.

'What was that?'

More sounds vibrated through the earth above and even Toby, intent as he had been on where her mouth was going next, was pulled back into the present. He sat up, resting on his elbows, and tilted his head sideways, listening. Petra knew he was hearing sounds she couldn't, the wolf in him commanding skills she never would.

'It sounds like . . .' he muttered, the words trailing

away as his eyes widened and his spine stiffened. 'It sounds like a thousand people all starting to move at the same time.' He looked down at her and she knew what he was going to say before he did.

'She's awake.'

'She *can't* be.' Petra's heart pounded as she grabbed at her clothes. 'The curse was for a hundred years.'

'Someone broke it before.' Toby pulled her in for a kiss before doing up his shirt. 'Looks like someone's done it again. Come on. We need to go.'

Leaving the love nest of the secret room behind, they went back out into the tunnels and pressed themselves into the shadows as the sound of grunting and wriggling came from the tunnel to their left, and then finally two men fell free of the thicket's roots, dressed in castle servant livery, and hurried back in the direction of their place of employment. Once they had vanished, Petra and Toby stared at the tunnel the two men had been trapped in. The roots were still very much there. Not as thick as they had been, but not gone.

'She's awake,' Petra said softly. 'But the curse isn't fully broken.'

'We can solve that riddle later,' Toby said, grabbing her hand. 'Let's find a way out. The baker's house is probably the safest. Then we'll see what's happened in this cursed kingdom. And pray the Beast doesn't wake too soon.'

They crept out through the baker's house before the man and his wife made it downstairs, and while Toby headed to the thicket to see if the prince or Rumpelstiltskin were back, Petra went to the castle, which had launched straight back into the wedding preparations even though people were mildly confused that it had been night only moments before. Others were hurriedly getting dressed, baffled that they'd slept so late, and from one room came a cry of, 'My rubies! Where have they gone?' and then the sound of a protesting maid declaring her innocence. After so many months of quiet, every sound was an assault, but Petra – despite the impending catastrophe of the Beast – was selfishly happy and excited that the world was awake around them once more. Maybe she would get a chance to talk to her grandmother again after all.

'The First Minister?' she asked a passing valet, weighed down with pressed doublets, as she tried to navigate the busy corridors. 'Where can I find him? Where are his rooms?'

***

BLOOD

The First Minister was clutching his head, a wine jug beside him, when Petra found him sitting at his desk in despair.

'*You*,' he said, eyes widening when he saw her. 'I thought you put her back to sleep.' Red wine dribbled into the crevices around his mouth as he took another swallow. 'Everything's ruined.'

'I did put her back to sleep,' she said. 'Nearly two years ago. Someone else has woken her.'

From the corridor outside she could hear people asking about the whereabouts of the charming prince – the groom for the upcoming wedding – confused as to why he wasn't in his rooms, preparing for the big day.

'And we have to put her back to sleep again,' Petra said. 'How many times will that spindle work?'

'We'll never know,' the First Minister muttered. 'The boy threw it into the fire. It's gone.' He looked up at her, a broken man. 'She's awake and that's that. It's over. We're all doomed.'

Eleven

The witch had been sitting in her rocking chair by the fire since before dawn, sipping mug after mug of nettle tea. The heat soothed the pain in her knuckles. It had been a long life, and although there were still plenty of years ahead, the heaviness of her bones was starting to take its toll. It wasn't the arthritis that disturbed her night this time. It was her dreams that had woken her, heart racing, gasping for breath. Dreams of an all-consuming fire, burning her up, the flames so hot they were as white as her hair. It was more than a dream, she'd known that as soon as her breathing steadied and panic faded in the cool, dark air. It was too rich for that, and her fingers prickled so much it became a maddening itch under her skin until she soaked her hands in cold water rather than let the magic fly, and then, as the irritation eased, the slow familiar throb in her knuckles took over.

No, it wasn't simply a dream. It was a promise. She could feel it. Something in the air had shifted. She got to her feet, wrapped a shawl around her and took her hot drink outside to study the early morning sky. This deep in the forest the mornings were always damp and dewy, clouds lingering low, the trees tightly packed and sparkling green, but today she could see the Far Mountain in the distance, and even the constant clouds there appeared to be burning off, heat from the dragon pit creating a shimmer in the air.

Her heart beat a little faster. They must be stirring, she decided. Sometimes she had flashes of seeing the Far Mountain as something much closer, tiny memories of her life before this one, in the world of pretty dresses and shining glass. The memories never lasted long, and even if they all came back to her, it was so long ago now it would be hard to see it as anything other than a dream.

She looked back at the peak in the distance. Even for her, after everything she'd seen and learned in her long life, she thought that maybe the dragons were also dreaming of their song to come. Pure magic from the Far Mountain itself. The thought alone was enough to give her a moment's awe. Stories were weaving together, humming harp strings in the air. Fate, even, for what was fate if not a satisfactory story?

As a squirrel darted across the clearing hunting for any dropped nuts, she broke a piece of gingerbread from the windowsill and tossed it to him, watching as he grabbed his treasure and dashed happily back to the comfort of the trees to share it with his mate and the two kits she knew were nesting in the crook of a tree close to the cottage.

Family. Could this sense that something was coming have anything to do with Lilith and Snow White, she wondered? More than likely. It had been a quiet year since they'd come to her cottage glowing with their true love and she'd been glad they'd finally found each other. Rage and bitterness were hard to hold on to, and in the long years since she'd built her cottage here, determined to get revenge on the boy who'd taken her body and left her with this one, even her own resentments had faded. She'd had a good life. Magic at her fingertips gave her a power she'd never have had as a noblewoman with fading beauty in a predominantly man's world. She'd had a daughter she'd loved, and a granddaughter who'd become Queen of the Winter Lands, and now, although that granddaughter had died of fever, she had her great-granddaughter, Lilith, a queen in her own right, whose rage and anger she'd recognised because it was so very like her own of old.

The witch had set her anger free a long time ago, once she'd realised it was escaping her, drip by drip over the years. The boy had never come back and would be long dead by now, no doubt. He'd been clever and smart and nimble and wicked, but his way of life would almost surely have guaranteed an early death. The body that was once hers, Rapunzel's body, had grown old and died far away in the village where she'd lived with Conrad, and the witch, Gretel, as even she now thought of herself, had never followed her there, close to her own homeland. She'd let go of that too. They were all gone, and yet here she was, still alive, still very much enjoying *being* alive despite the aches and pains, and, if her senses were correct, with more adventures ahead of her.

Birds tweeted at each other, cooing in the morning, as a woodpecker hammered out his tune. Everything seemed calm in the forests and the kingdoms, and maybe it was, but still, she had an unsettled feeling in her waters. Glancing back towards the cloudless Far Mountain, she thought perhaps the long-hidden dragons did too.

Her hands were steadier now but her feet itched and, once she'd finished her tea, she packed herself a bag of provisions and pulled on her walking boots.

She didn't take any weapon to defend herself for she didn't fear walking through the forests. She was Gretel the witch and there was no one – man nor creature – who could challenge her.

Her heart picked up speed as she felt a sudden rush of anticipation. It would be good to see Lilith again. It was always nice to visit family, and she had a feeling that perhaps her great-granddaughter might once again need her help.

She sucked in a deep breath of fresh air and, with a contented smile, started to walk.

Twelve

'What are you doing here?' The young queen, clad only in a white, lace-trimmed nightdress, stared at Aladdin, confused and worried as she quickly pulled a pink silk robe around herself. Her eyes were still hazy and as she spoke it was as if she was struggling to find the words. 'Why are you in my bedchamber? And where are my maids?'

'I'm Aladdin. A traveller. You were bleeding.' He looked down at the floor and, following his gaze, her eyes widened. She looked aghast as she saw the pool of blood beside her pale, delicate feet. 'I stopped it.'

'Again?' she said, looking at her pricked finger, and tears sprang to her eyes. 'With the spindle? But why? And how long this time?' She burst into tears, soft sobs shaking her shoulders, and Aladdin's fingers itched to take out his knife and slit her throat.

'I don't know. I threw the spindle into the fire. It's gone.' He took a pastry from his pocket and offered it to her. 'You should eat something, Your Majesty. For the shock.' He didn't like this pathetically sweet girl, but if she was the queen then he wanted to be her friend, at least until he was safely out of the castle and back at the thicket. He was going to be in trouble with the huntsman for this – the warning to stay away from the castle very much now in the forefront of his mind – and maybe this queen would be useful.

'How do I know I can trust you?' she asked and Aladdin almost laughed aloud. One look at her doe eyes and he knew this woman trusted everyone. Oh, to be himself again here, unrestrained by lamps and magic. He'd have her eating out of the palm of his hand and he'd be able to do as he pleased.

'Did you once have a friend called Rapunzel?' he asked.

'Yes,' she smiled and then frowned. 'I loved her. When I was little and I had Domino, my precious cat. Before he vanished.' Her hand went to her head as if it was suddenly throbbing. 'I can't remember exactly. My head feels strange.'

'I knew her too. She lived with a witch.'

'She left before I went to sleep last time. More than a hundred years ago. It was her father, Uncle Rumple, who brought the spindle ...' More tears fell, and Aladdin put his arm around her.

'You're not the only one who has fallen foul of magic,' he said. 'A witch put a spell on me too. And I knew Rapunzel. She was my friend. I know she missed you even though the witch stopped her remembering her old life properly. Sometimes she dreamed of you and she said you were her best friend.' He paused, his own dark eyes echoing the soft expression of her own. 'And then I was.'

'Well,' the young woman forced a smile through her tears. 'If Rapunzel loved you, then I shall too. My name is Beauty. I am the queen and this is the Kingdom of Light and Glass. The man who was in here is my First Minister.' Her bottom lip wobbled again.

'The spindle was in his lap when I found you. I've seen cursed spindles before and that's why I burned it.'

Beauty took both his hands, holding them tightly. 'And for that, I'm forever grateful. But why would he want to curse me like that? On the night before my wedding.' Her eyes widened as if she'd totally forgotten her marriage until the words came out of her mouth. 'The prince! He'll be looking for me!'

She darted to the locked door and rattled the handles. 'Let me out! I command you!' She hammered at the door. 'Please! I must see the prince! My love!'

When no one answered she flopped on the bed, her tears flowing once more, and Aladdin wondered how his spirited Rapunzel had ever been friends with such a wet blanket. As she wept, he went to the door and pressed a water glass against it, listening carefully. The castle was very much alive, and amidst all the other noise, he heard voices looking for the prince, confused. They weren't going to find a prince, Aladdin was becoming quite sure about that.

'Is today your wedding day?' he asked, as her sobs grew more grating. 'Perhaps they're preparing a surprise for you. Maybe that's why he needed you to be asleep.' He said it so reasonably it was almost convincing. 'It's probably something like that rather than anything sinister. Perhaps the prince had to return to his kingdom for a year or more and didn't want you to miss him as much as he must miss you, so allowed you to sleep through it.'

'Do you really think so?' Beauty sat up, sniffing and wiping her eyes.

'Of course. It would be awful to have to wait a year, wouldn't it?'

'Oh yes. I can't bear to be away from him. He's the

most handsome and charming prince a queen could wish to marry.'

'Tell me all about him,' Aladdin said, and before she'd even taken a breath he'd mentally switched off from listening, and, as she gushed about their whirlwind romance, he made occasional noises of approval and encouragement and looked around for some kind of clue as to how she had ended up in this predicament.

It was only when he reached her drawer of perfumes that he found something intriguing, and in fact he very nearly missed it. He'd glanced in quickly and had been about to close the drawer again, the rush of sweet, floral scents making him nauseous, when a small, dark bottle at the back caught his eyes. The rest were daintily cut crystal vials filled with pale liquids, but this one, half the size and more like a small apothecary bottle, sat in the shadows like a secret. He took it out and carefully opened it, holding it under his nose. Unripe tomatoes. Slightly bitter. This wasn't perfume, this was poison. Belladonna. Deadly nightshade. Suddenly this simpering girl was becoming more interesting. Was all this sweetness simply an act? Was this pretty, pastel queen in fact a tyrant?

'This doesn't seem like something you'd have,' he said, casually, turning to face her.

'That?' She frowned, peering closer. 'That's only vanilla essence. It's for making apple pie. It makes it taste better.'

'I suppose it *is* flavouring of a sort, but it's not vanilla.' Aladdin looked down at the bottle and then up at her with a wry smile. 'Anyone who ate that apple pie wouldn't last very long.'

'Don't be silly. I used it in pies for my father, the king. I loved him very much and he loved apples.' She sat up, staring at something and nothing in front of her, her fingers twitching. 'I made him so many pies.' One of her hands suddenly flew to her face, her fingers tapping hard at her cheek. 'But I don't want to think about that. It's not good to think about that. It's only flavouring.' She got to her feet and hurried to the door, rattling the handles. 'I need to get out of here. Away from that bottle. I need some fresh air. Why would you show me that?'

Aladdin watched, fascinated, as her face contorted into something close to vicious anger and she banged harder on the door.

'I demand that you let me out! I am your queen!' She pulled her foot back and kicked hard.

Aladdin leaned back against the dresser. Maybe, finally, this was getting interesting.

Thirteen

Toby moved as fast as he could to the thicket, occasionally feigning the yawns he saw in those around him who were quickly joining the day after so much slumber. Some residents would be waking to missing laundry and other items that he and Petra had taken for their own home, and at least the cries of thievery might keep the guards occupied for a while.

The residents in the castle had woken first and the partial lifting of the curse moved outwards like a ripple in water as one by one the streets were brought out of their slumber. By the time he reached the thicket, the whole kingdom was once again alert, and the thick wall of briars and vines trembled as it shrank. Was the sleep finally over? Would they all be free? It was an exciting thought. He could leave with Petra and never come back. His own curse might be for life, but they could go somewhere where his secret was safer. Live in the Fae Forest, or maybe even further away. A quiet place where his monthly changes wouldn't terrify locals.

But while the thicket had thinned and dropped several feet in height, it had not disappeared. He stayed hidden until the grunts of guards – who'd been trapped inside when the prince and the huntsman fled – stopped and they'd wriggled themselves free.

'They got away,' one muttered.

'We should go back. Tell the First Minister.'

They pulled on their helmets and started towards the castle, as yet unaware that any time had passed at all. As soon as they were gone, Toby jogged further up to see what looked like a fox hole at the base of the thicket. He crouched, peering inside. Just like in the tunnels below, the roots were still thick and impassable. As before, the enchantment might be half-lifted but there was still magic trapping them all inside.

'Huntsman?' he called out, trying to pull apart the branches of the thicket to call through, but they were too strong. 'Are you there?'

'Toby? You can hear me?'

'Yes!' Toby grinned as a cloud cut across the bright summer's day, making the breeze suddenly chilly. 'What brings you back here causing trouble?'

'Another problem of royal making. When there's time for wine, I'll tell you everything, but for now I have to get you out of there. I need your help.'

'Not sure about the getting out part, but I owe you a service so tell me what you need.'

It was good to hear the huntsman's voice again. He'd liked his honest forest ways and enjoyed his wit. He was a friend, and he was glad to have the chance to talk to him again. In many ways, he realised he was glad the queen was awakened. He'd already lived one hundred years in the sleeping city with only Rumpelstiltskin for company and while he knew he could do one hundred more, he didn't want that for Petra. People needed people, he knew that, and he wanted Petra to have more than just him.

'Did Aladdin find you?' The huntsman's voice was faint but clear.

'Aladdin? Who is that?' He paused. 'Is he the one who's woken Beauty?'

'He's done *what*?'

'The kingdom is awake again,' Toby said. 'That's why I came here.' He looked back, as if he could somehow show the huntsman the lively city through the thick plants, and his eyes widened. Dark clouds were forming in the sky, tendrils of deep grey, like smoke, joining up and weaving together into thick, black masses overhead, blocking out the sun and threatening sudden night.

'Oh, no,' he muttered, before looking back at the thicket and adding more loudly, 'we have a problem.'

'What?' the huntsman called through, concerned. 'What is it?'

'Black clouds,' he said, just as the first tiny shard of blue lightning cracked across the sky and a low thunder rumbled after it. 'I think the Beast is coming.'

***

'We have to kill her.'

Petra watched as the First Minister paced his rooms, clutching his wine, the afternoon sunlight dappling now with clouds. He was agitated but she knew better than to try to calm him down. He needed to get the shock out of his system and make peace with his own decisions and then he'd be level-headed again. He wouldn't have survived long under Beauty and the Beast if he wasn't a skilled politician.

'*I* have to kill her,' he continued as he stopped in his tracks. He sat back down, heavily, suddenly looking a lot older, and put his glass down too. 'It's the only way. The kingdom can't go on like this, with bouts of cruelty and bloodlust and murder. The depravity of the Beast. She makes cruelty acceptable and that cannot be. That is not who we are.'

'How will you do it?' Petra's mouth dried. Despite what she knew of the Beast she still felt so sorry for poor Beauty, living unaware of the terror she inspired when she was the Beast.

'A painless poison, if the apothecary can find me one. And I will need a trustworthy apothecary. I think I know the right man. He knows the truth about the Beast. He will understand.'

'Are you sure it's the only way?' Petra asked, and he let out a long sigh and then straightened his shoulders.

'It is only a quicker version of what we tried with the spindle. I have had her death on my hands for a very long time, even if it has yet to come to pass. I will do it myself. Both Beauty and the Beast trust me, so when I give it to her she won't suspect anything. I'll taste it myself if I have to, to give her confidence in it. There would be some justice in that.'

'What will you tell people? When she dies? Surely no one will believe that such a young and healthy queen could die naturally so quickly?'

'The prince is gone. The whole castle is looking for him. If I do it quickly I can say he killed her. She's locked up so no one will know it wasn't him. There will be demands for war but then we will unite in grief. If she doesn't make me drink the poison first, I can rule until such time as the nobles decide who has the best claim.'

It was nearly evening but it suddenly seemed unnaturally dark outside. Only then did Petra look out of the window. Black storm clouds had gathered, ominous and thick as soot. Before she could speak the warning that gripped her gut, a low rumble of thunder, the growl of a wild animal, made the air tremble. She looked back at the First Minister and saw her own fear reflected on his face.

'Oh, no,' he breathed as a flash of blue lightning cut across the sky. 'The Beast. She's here.'

'You said there was a boy with her?' Petra leapt to her feet. 'The one who woke her? He won't be safe.'

'He's old enough to be left to his fate. Eighteen perhaps. And you can't do anything now.' The First Minister grabbed at her arm. 'It's too dangerous! I'll tell the soldiers to kill her on sight if they can, but we have to let her be. To do whatever she wants. I can't risk her wrath if this goes wrong. The soldiers I could blame somehow on the prince. You and I? We have to wait for Beauty to return.'

'I'm going to find that young man,' Petra said, pulling her arm free. 'Beauty and the Beast are your problem. I only want to know why someone woke her. And I need to make sure she doesn't hurt him.'

Fourteen

Aladdin stared at Beauty as she kicked harder at the door, her face a tight scowl, delicate hands curled into bloodless fists. As dark clouds blotted the sunshine and a rumble of thunder brewed in the distance, he found it wasn't her anger that he couldn't drag his eyes away from. It was her hair.

There was a crackle of something in the air, as if it was suddenly heavier, and as a flash of blue lightning split the sky, her hair started to *change*. The colours were reversing, each strand transforming as if some dyed liquid was being poured over her head.

Her black, glossy locks were turning blonde, and the blonde stripes at either side of her sweet face were turning black. Even the way she held herself was different. There was something animal about her now, a hungry, prowling panther instead of a happy, joyful dove. Just as her hair transformation was complete, somewhere outside a bell started tolling, ringing out across the city. Aladdin wasn't sure if it was his imagination but the sounds of the city changed too – as if every citizen was rushing for home – and then there was quiet once more.

'That bell is always ringing when I wake up,' Beauty said, irritated, rattling the door handle again.

When she turned towards him, her eyes wandering over him as if he were potential prey, it made his skin tingle. It was strange. As if he was facing an entirely different person.

'Who dared to lock me in here?' she asked, her tone light but deadly. 'They'll go straight to the dungeons.' She stepped closer. 'Which is where you should go for being in my bedchamber uninvited.'

'Don't you remember who locked us in?' Aladdin asked.

'I was asleep. And if I remembered I wouldn't have to ask.' She stepped closer still, sleek and dangerous, and purred, 'And if you answer me with a question again I'll cut your tongue out and eat it, pretty boy.'

'I'll bear that in mind, Your Majesty,' he said with a smile. Whatever had happened to Beauty, this version of her was far more intriguing than the sweet, cloying fool who'd first woken up. 'I believe it was your First Minister. He was asleep in that chair when I arrived and bandaged your finger. There was a spindle. I burnt it.'

She looked around her, thoughtful. 'I hate this room. These colours. I won't be spending my wedding night here.' She looked at him again, as if only just remembering he was there, and under her gaze his heart, always so cool and steady, picked up its pace. It was a very odd sensation indeed. 'Where is the prince? Are you one of his valets?' She smiled and tilted her head, studying him. 'Or are you a wedding gift?' She touched his cheek, and his heart raced faster. 'Perhaps a return present for the dead wench's blood?'

'I am nobody's gift, although the dead wench business sounds like a story I'd like to hear over a glass of wine,' he answered, their faces only inches apart. Her lips were full and red against her pale skin. She was dangerous, all his senses told him that, wicked right down to her core. She'd kill him as soon as look at him, and she'd enjoy it. He had never met such a girl before. She reminded him of himself and he hadn't thought another like him existed. 'But the prince fled the castle while you slept. And I don't want to be the bearer of bad news but you should probably know – your First Minister was trying to kill you.'

'He wouldn't dare.' She stepped back, her eyes narrowing.

'The other one didn't believe me either.'

'Other one?' She frowned, as if with the pang of a sharp momentary headache, and turned away.

Aladdin stared at her as she shrugged off the pink silk robe and went to the wardrobe, pushing all the beautiful pastel dresses to one side and reaching far into the back, so far she almost stepped inside, before taking out a black satin dress with a dark red velvet triangle running across the chest and down to the waistline. She slipped out of her nightdress and stood naked for a moment, completely at ease in her nudity, before pulling the delicate fabric over her head and letting it ripple like water down her form, clinging to her curves. For the first time in his life, Aladdin felt himself respond to a naked woman's body and his face burned with heat and desire. It was so peculiar he nearly had to sit down. What was happening to him? Why was his heart racing? Was he about to die?

'What do you mean *other* one?' She opened a drawer of her dressing table and took something from underneath it – a beautiful knife made of the best dwarf steel with rubies set into its hilt. She slid it into the red velvet of her dress, hiding it there. Aladdin's heart beat even faster. She was the strangest creature, so opposite to the Beauty who he'd first awoken. 'You must have seen a serving girl. Or a maid.'

How could she be so different? And not remember what they'd spoken of? Aladdin held up the poison bottle. 'I have to ask – do you know what this is?'

'Why don't you drink some and see?' She smiled again and he loved the way her teeth looked so white and sharp.

'Belladonna is not to my taste,' he answered smoothly. 'Although I am a fan of its usage. I take it this is how you got rid of your father, the king?'

'Is that why the First Minister tried to kill me?' Her voice was honey thick and straight from the hive. 'Are you his spy?' She walked past him and picked up a jewellery box sitting high on a shelf of cat ornaments made from glass and ceramic and stone. 'Should I send him back your liver?'

'I'd rather you left my liver where it is,' he said. 'And no, I'm not his spy. I'm not from this kingdom, I'm not your enemy, and we actually have quite a lot in common.'

'I doubt that,' she muttered, opening the lid and ignoring the tinkling music that played as a ballerina doll spun inside. She lifted out the pink false bottom of the box and retrieved a key.

'I murdered my father too,' he said, and she paused

on her way back to the locked door, glancing over her shoulder at him, curious, as if he might be more interesting than she first thought. Her eyes were almost hazy, as if she was permanently in the grip of lust.

It made his stomach flip. He had never seen the appeal in sex. The way Rapunzel had wanted the young king seemed like a weakness to him. But now, looking at this *other* Beauty, his mouth was dry and his palms sweating.

'And my mother. Sliced both their throats,' he continued, before adding, 'brutally,' remembering the mess of those first kills. 'There was so much blood. It was my fault. I got carried away and nearly decapitated my father. It wasn't the sharpest of blades either.' He winked at her. 'I've learned a lot since then.'

'You like blood?' She slid the key into the lock and turned it.

'I like spilling it.'

'Then you might be useful to me after all.'

Fifteen

The huntsman was becoming more and more frustrated with his efforts to hack through the thicket. While it had definitely shrunk there was no getting through to the other side. The vines and flowers grew back the moment he cut them, and every time he pressed through a foot or so, they rallied and pushed him back out. The magical hedge might have let the soldiers out once they had woken, but it was absolutely not letting the huntsman *in*.

The hot afternoon sun was setting now in the clear sky overhead, and while birds chirped merrily in the woods behind them and butterflies darted here and there, he knew it was very different for Toby on the other side. In the occasional glimpses he managed to get of the kingdom beyond the branches he could see the land was in the grip of a storm, the sky blackened with thunder clouds and flashes of blue lightning. If it was hard work for him here in the calm summer afternoon, then Toby must really be struggling. They'd given up trying to talk to each other as the noise of the storm meant Toby couldn't hear him, and despite having hacked at the bushes for over an hour, they were no further forward than when they started.

'It's no use,' Dreamy said, breathless, as Bolshy pulled Feisty and then him free of the muddy earth. 'We can't dig under, the roots keep growing.'

'It's like a pit of snakes.' Feisty threw down his shovel, annoyed. 'You move one, and it comes straight back at you, stronger and angrier.'

'Same up here.'

'I don't understand it,' Dreamy sat back on the grass, confused. 'If the curse has been broken and the queen is awake, then why is the thicket still here?'

The huntsman took a swig of dwarf ale and then passed the gourd around. He knew the answer. He knew it from the curse he'd been placed under by Lilith when she'd turned him from man to mouse.

'There's only one cure for a curse,' he muttered. If they couldn't find a way through the hedge, or Petra couldn't find a way to get them out from that side, then perhaps the foolish prince would have to give up his child after all.

The sun finally burned orange-gold, saying its farewell for the day as it sank down below the horizon. Now he was sure he could just about make out the sound of the storm.

How could there ever be a cure for *that* curse? It couldn't be possible. *Could* it?

***

'What are you looking for?'

Lilith was high up the library ladder, pulling out the four books she'd hidden amidst the thousands of leather volumes the old king would never read. It had been so long she'd almost forgotten where she'd put them, but as soon as her pale fingers brushed across their spines, the contents sang out to her. She had three beside her on the top step and her fingers tingled as she touched the fourth, almost giddy when she pulled the faded red tome from the shelf and added it to the others.

'What do you think I'm looking for in a library?' She smiled down at Snow before carefully putting the heavy books in the bag across her shoulder and climbing the twenty feet or more back down the polished mahogany ladder to the floor. 'A pair of shoes?'

'Very funny,' Snow said, kissing her. 'I didn't know where you were when I got back from riding. The cook said you were in here and you didn't want dinner. It sounded like the old days when you were married to my father. I left you alone as long as possible but it's night and you must be hungry.' She nodded towards the tray she'd deposited on a leather-topped desk. 'Red wine, cheese and fresh bread.'

'I'm sorry.' Lilith sat on a soft, velvet reading couch nearest the unlit fireplace and put the books beside her. 'I lost track of time. A raven arrived with a message from my great-grandmother. She's coming to see us. She said she had a dream of fire. A fire so bright and hot it could only be one thing.'

Snow sat beside her, eyes widening. 'Dragon song?'

'Perhaps.'

The excitement in Snow's eyes both worried her and made her smile in equal measure. She was beautiful, kind *and* fearless. It was the last that sometimes made Lilith afraid. Snow hadn't seen the things Lilith had. The cruelties of the world. She'd never lived in fear in the way Lilith had as a child, her mother's books and true nature hidden away. Even during that dark period with the prince and Lilith pushing her away,

Snow had always believed the best of people. That good would win over evil and true love conquered all and lovers would live happily ever after. But she'd never heard the screams at a burning. She didn't have witch's blood. And if anything made Lilith happy it was knowing that Snow would never bear that burden. Snow White was everything good in the world and she made Lilith a better person for it.

'I'm not sure. But she thinks they're stirring. The clouds are going from the Far Mountain.'

'I saw that when I was riding. I thought it was a trick of the sunlight. What would wake them?' Snow sat beside her, curious now, opening one of the old books, the spine creaking with age and lack of use, and looking at the dense, elaborate writing and illustrations on the first few pages.

'Hopefully these books will tell us. My mother used to say that dragons know when they're needed. Perhaps they sense a summoning is coming.'

'This must be to do with the prince?' Snow looked up. 'And Rumpelstiltskin's demands?'

'Or maybe it's nothing to do with us. There is much magic in the kingdoms, and many stories being told and lived.'

Snow snorted a laugh. 'If your great-grandmother is on the way then it's to do with us. She wouldn't leave her cottage if she didn't think you needed her help. I remember her face when you asked if she wanted to live with us.'

Lilith remembered it well. The disgust on her great-grandmother's face at the thought of living on the palace grounds. *In another time and another place, I would have been happy to. But no longer.* Perhaps she'd regretted letting Lilith's mother marry the King of the Winter Lands despite her mother's insistence that he loved her. Her great-grandmother held no truck with royals, and she'd known nothing of the Winter Lands and the terrible price paid there by witches for their magic. Not until she'd gone to her granddaughter's wedding.

She'd made sure Lilith was not so naïve though. She'd trained her well in the duplicity of men and how to play for power. Only when Lilith had realised how much she loved Snow, and her own ice heart had melted, did she wonder who had hurt her great-grandmother so much that for so many years under her cheerful exterior she had constantly been curating an archive of revenge, just in case one was needed.

'She'll be here by morning,' Lilith said. 'All will be clear then. Or before, if I can find some answers in one of these books.'

'By morning?' Snow moved closer to her on the couch. 'That's not so very far away.' She moved closer still, putting the book she'd opened down on the floor. 'And when she's here she always sleeps in the room next to us.' With a teasing smile, she leaned forwards and then Lilith felt her soft, red lips, gentle against her neck, her breath warm as her hot tongue flicked against Lilith's skin. She moaned, she couldn't help herself.

'I need to work,' she whispered, as Snow's body pressed against hers and pushed her further back onto the soft velvet.

'Work can wait,' Snow said, before kissing her, long and full, one hand slipping under the satin of her dress. 'I'm going to show you a fire as white and hot as any dragon song.' As her fingers slid into Lilith's underwear and found the wetness there, all thought of magic and dragons and curses was lost in the fireworks in her mind.

'Yes,' she moaned as she pulled Snow closer to her, pushing herself against her lover's fingers, hungrily undoing the buttons of Snow's shirt, her mouth and hands eager for her full breasts. 'Set me on fire, my love.'

And as they writhed and moaned and lost themselves in each other, in the distance, under the blanket of night, in the cauldron of the Far Mountain itself, a dragon stirred in its sleep.

Sixteen

Hidden behind a thick, red, velvet curtain, the young queen had opened a heavy iron door, and Aladdin quickly followed her to the stairway beyond, wiping the splatter of blood from his face. He couldn't help but be impressed at how efficiently she'd dealt with four soldiers since their escape from her rooms, and just now slit the throat of a fat baker they'd come across as he was shoving half a dozen silver spoons into his pocket, guilt at his thievery writ large on his red face.

'You murder very elegantly,' Aladdin said as she led them down into the darkness of the dungeons. Torches flared alight as she passed – and for a moment he was reminded of Rapunzel's tower, where the torches also lit themselves, and he realised that he and this mad queen had more in common than their bloodlust. They had both lived a lot longer than most and if they were to be out in the other kingdoms again they would no doubt find it a changed world. But still, it was her skill with the blade that had made his heart race.

'And yet it appears that despite your own claims, you don't murder at all,' she purred, turning and holding her blade against the corner of his mouth. 'So why am I keeping you alive?'

Rather than threatening she sounded almost puzzled by her choice not to end him then and there. Close up, Aladdin found her even more mesmerising, despite – or perhaps because of – the threats she made against him. She'd been so efficient in despatching her victims that she and her clothes were clean of blood except for the streak on the glinting metal. Aladdin let his tongue run along it, tasting the cooling metallic warmth. He'd never voluntarily tasted blood before, other than the occasional accident, and, as he cleaned the knife of the fat baker's remains, he was quite sure he wouldn't want a mouthful of it, but for some reason he was keen to impress her.

'As I already explained, I'm under a spell. I can only fight back if my life or another's is under threat and even then I can only wound or disarm.' Her eyes were flecked with violet and close up her skin was perfectly smooth. He felt an overwhelming urge to touch her. 'I wish you could see me at my best. There's nothing I'd like more than to show you my skills.' He glanced sideways, suddenly distracted by the equipment in the cell beside him. A long wooden table with wrist and ankle straps. 'I take it this is all your work? It doesn't look like something the other one would like.' He paused, studying the pulley system. 'Does that stretch people?'

'Yes.' She lowered the knife an inch. 'A rack. I like to remove fingernails at the same time. They think they've screamed all they can, but they can always find more.' Her voice had lowered to a breathy whisper and her face flushed. 'I feel warm thinking about it.' She looked at him sideways and every inch of his skin tingled. 'Don't you?'

He wanted to mutter his agreement but was struggling to get his voice to work, when he suddenly saw something move in the shadows behind her. A dark shape and then the flash of a sword being drawn.

He moved on instinct, as fast as a dart, nimble fingers straight onto the nerve in her wrist so that the blade dropped from her hand to his, and then he spun her round and out of the way as he pulled his own knife free. As the soldier, a thick-bodied thug of a man, lunged all his bodyweight forward, Aladdin dropped and slid across the floor, his feet taking the soldier's out from under him, knives slashing at both heels, cutting deep through the leather of his boots to reach the tendons beneath, severing one with each sharp blade before bouncing back to his own feet. His breath still even, he looked down, satisfied, as the man screamed in agony on the dirty floor.

'I can't kill him, sadly,' he said, holding out the knives to the queen. 'But please, do the honours. Although perhaps it would be more fun to leave him like this? It's filthy down here and no doubt he'll get an infection and die more slowly that way.'

She came forward, her blonde hair shining under the torchlight, and for the first time since they'd met he saw something in her eyes that set his heart on fire. Recognition. Awe. Perhaps even a sense of homecoming.

'You really are like me,' she said softly, in the voice that seemed always on the edge of murder or lust. 'Others try to be. To please me. And some come close.' She traced a finger down his cheek and once again he felt sensations in his body that he had never thought were for him. He wanted to touch her. He wanted to be with her constantly. He wanted to—

And then she kissed him. Her lips were soft and warm and he couldn't help but moan as her tongue darted into his mouth and his own chased hers back. His whole body trembled as his arms slid around her waist and the injured man's cries of pain excited them both as they pulled each other closer, eager for more.

As they kissed, something shifted around them. At first he thought it was only him, the strangeness of these new emotions making it feel as if the whole world was changing, but the gloomy dungeon corridor shimmered with light and the earth beneath their feet shook as if the Far Mountain itself was rumbling and dragons were waking to sing. The very air around them felt lighter, but as they broke apart, all he could see was her. His blonde-haired love.

'You really are a beauty,' he breathed, staring at her. 'The other one doesn't compare.'

'I'm the only one who matters.'

She leaned in to kiss him again but this time bit down hard on his lip, her sharp teeth cutting into his soft flesh. As he gasped with the surprise pain, she stepped back, smiling, her lips redder as she licked his blood from them.

'I wanted to taste you just once,' she murmured, as full of lust as he was.

He pulled her back to him and kissed her once more, his mouth tangy with the taste of his own blood, and then sheathed his knife and took her hand. 'We should get out of here. More soldiers will come. Much as it would be fun to despatch them, I'd rather we were free of this castle for now.'

***

They'd made it into the next corridor when she stopped dead, frozen to the spot. Aladdin turned and tried to hurry her along but she looked right through him, her expression confused. 'I think the blood does it,' she muttered, almost to herself. 'I forget every time but I think it's the blood. It sends me back inside.'

'What are you talking about?' As he asked the question, the answer began to present itself. Her hair – her beautiful blonde hair with the black stripes – was starting to change again, the colours bleeding together before slowly separating out in reverse.

'No, no, *no*.' He grabbed her arms, horrified, shaking her. 'Stop it! Come back!'

But even as his fingers dug hard into her skin he could see she was lost. The golden-yellow hair had retreated back to the two strands around her pale face and the rest was glossy black.

'What am I doing here?' Beauty said, bleary eyes looking around the dungeon. 'What is this awful place?' She looked down, aghast. 'And what happened to this poor soldier? We have to help him!'

'Don't you remember?' Aladdin pressed her. 'Anything at all?' How could she be so different? Once again he felt revulsion at the sweetness that emanated from the young queen – the Beauty – in front of him. While he knew his own nature wasn't quite right, he knew that neither was hers. Two souls trapped in one body, and he knew which one he preferred.

'Oh, thank god, you're all right.'

Aladdin looked up, knife immediately drawn, to see a pretty woman with strawberry blonde hair hurrying towards them.

'You,' Beauty said, looking at her, still hazy with confusion. 'Petra. You came with the prince. Where is he? Do you know why I'm here? I woke up in my bedroom and it was locked. Then I don't know what happened but I found myself here, still with this boy.'

'I'm a young man, actually.' The sooner this one left and the other one came back the better. 'And not all that young if you're counting in years.'

'We'll find him,' the woman said, and then turned her attention to Aladdin and dropped her voice. 'Where did you come from? Did you wake her up? Was the Beast here?'

'The Beast?' His grip on the knife tightened. 'If you mean—'

'The thicket!' Shouts from further along the corridor and out in the castle cut him off. 'It's shrinking!'

'They'll kill her if they find her.' The woman grabbed Aladdin with one hand and Beauty with the other. 'If the thicket is shrinking, then I know a way out.'

'I'm supposed to be getting married,' Beauty whimpered as Petra pulled them past all the cells and rounded the corner, sneaking them out of another iron door and back into the castle. 'That's better,' Beauty said then, as they came out into the dining room, where so many candles were lit that it looked like daylight. 'I was getting an awful headache in there. Everything feels so strange.'

'They normally make sure she becomes herself again in her bedroom,' Petra said to Aladdin as she crouched by the large, unlit fireplace and tugged at the fixings at the back. 'No wonder she's so distressed.'

'Maybe this one isn't *herself*. Maybe the other one has just as much right to exist. Have you considered that?'

Petra looked at him and then down at his blood-stained knife. 'I'm thinking I probably didn't need to worry about your safety with her. Did she hurt the soldier or was it you?'

A door swung open before he could answer and she hurried Aladdin and the young queen through onto some stairs that led to an underground network of narrow spaces and unadorned corridors.

'Are these thieves' tunnels?' Aladdin's eyes narrowed. 'They look like a smuggler's work.'

'No one would steal from the castle,' Beauty said, hurt. 'My people are good people. They look after each other and we live well.'

'A whole kingdom of goodness?' Aladdin laughed as they rounded another corner. 'How very dull. And a fiction. There can be no such thing.' He looked at her sideways. 'You of all people should be aware that for every good there is a bad.'

'Why should I know that? You speak in riddles I don't understand.' She looked around her. 'Where is my prince?'

'We're going to find him,' Petra said, smiling reassuringly at her. 'It's an adventure.'

Finally they came to a halt in front of a tunnel where roots were wriggling back upwards, diminishing to nothing, as if perhaps they'd never been there at all.

Petra stared and then looked at Aladdin and Beauty. 'I have to ask. Did you two kiss?'

Seventeen

'The storm's gone.' Toby's voice was clear through the hedge. 'The night's clear again. But, something . . . something's different.'

The huntsman didn't need Toby to tell him changes were happening, he could *see* it. Above him, the endless thicket was folding in on itself, each layer vanishing as it turned, shrinking faster and faster with every second.

'What's happening?' said Feisty, staring upwards.

'The roots are disappearing too!' Dreamy called out from his seat on the lip of the tunnel.

'The curse has been broken,' the huntsman said as Toby came into view on the other side, although he couldn't for the life of him figure out how. There was only one thing that could break a curse and there was no way Beauty could have found it so quickly. Especially not when she'd been the Beast.

Torches flared in the night behind Toby and as the last of the thicket vanished, they grew closer.

'Who's coming after you?' the huntsman asked, pulling the wolf man into a hug, happy to see him again.

'Soldiers, I presume. Why did you send someone in there to wake Beauty?'

'I didn't. In fact I told him to stay away from the castle entirely, but I don't think he's made for following rules.'

'I hope he survived the Beast. And I hope Petra found them.'

'If anyone can deal with the Beast, it's Aladdin.'

The ground trembled under them, the shudder of horses heading their way, riding fast.

'We may need to be ready to fight. Or run.' He looked to the dwarves. 'Perhaps you should go and wait in the trees. Where you can't be seen.'

'Dwarves don't run.' Feisty stood proud alongside him, and pulled a small dagger from his belt.

'And we don't ever abandon our friends,' Dreamy added, gripping his shovel like a weapon.

The huntsman smiled down at them. 'You're good men. I can always use the help of good men.'

'It's a full moon,' Toby said softly, and as he looked up at the sky, the yellow flecks in his green eyes began to sparkle, bright against his black skin.

The huntsman looked at the line of soldiers coming towards them, followed by men on horses. He grinned. 'I can also always use the help of a good wolf.'

'We made it in time.'

The huntsman turned to see Petra, Aladdin and Beauty climbing up through a door hidden under the moss just within the first line of trees. As Beauty looked around, confused, Petra strode forward.

'They're coming for Beauty. The First Minister means to kill her.' She touched Toby's arm. 'I'll see you in the morning, my love.' They smiled at each other and then myriad lights glittered not only in Toby's eyes but all over his skin and, as Petra stepped back and the dwarves gasped and huddled closer together, the glittering colours, like a million tiny fireflies, rose and spun around him like a whirlwind until they were one solid block of light so bright it was as though lightning filled the entire night's sky.

The huntsman flinched and closed his eyes against the burning brightness. He didn't open them again until he heard a low growl and snuffle, and found Toby transformed into the vast wolf. The creature padded over to Petra, and as she pushed her fingers into its thick fur, it rubbed its face against her leg.

'Is everyone in this kingdom cursed?' Aladdin asked, dryly. 'I'm starting to feel less than special.'

'I told you not to go near the castle.' The huntsman glared at him.

'You also told me that these two would come when I called. They didn't.'

'He's right, we didn't hear him. We were underground,' Petra said. 'In the tunnels we just used to escape.'

'Why are we running away?' Beauty asked as Dreamy took off his coat so she could sit on it and Feisty gave her a cup of dwarf ale. The huntsman remembered the water witch magic Beauty had that made people be kind to her. Watching the soldiers getting closer – he could hear them now – he wondered if that magic was finally running out. 'And the thicket has gone. I'm glad about that. It didn't belong here. Did the prince make it go?'

'You didn't answer my question,' Petra said, looking at Aladdin, and the huntsman knew it was going to be the same question on the tip of his own tongue. 'Did you two kiss?'

'No!' Aladdin and Beauty spoke in unison, equally appalled.

'Only true love's kiss can break a curse,' the huntsman said. 'Trust me, I know.'

'I kissed the *other* one,' Aladdin said, and as they stared at him, shocked, the huntsman burst into hearty laughter.

'Well, perhaps then I can't be too angry that you went to the castle. Fate will not be fought, after all.'

'The Beast?' Petra said. 'You kissed *her?*'

'I don't want to interrupt, but we have company approaching.'

Feisty was right. The soldiers were nearly upon them, free from the streets and lanes of the city and heading towards the line of trees. At their head, the First Minister was visible in the torchlight, in all his robes, astride his horse, his face stern and committed.

'What did you mean, the other one?' Beauty asked, but no one answered. There wasn't time, and there was no need for Beauty to hear the truth of who she was from them, the huntsman thought.

'We can clear up this misunderstanding,' he said, as the group of soldiers, perhaps twenty in total, came to a halt, lances in hand, in front of him.

'We want our queen back,' the First Minister said as he climbed down from his horse. 'Quickly and quietly.'

'Of course. You know we've never meant your kingdom any harm.'

'Actually, *not* of course.' Petra stepped up, the growling wolf at her side. 'We're taking her with us.'

Beauty had got to her feet and been happily hurrying to the First Minister, but Petra held out her arm, blocking her, and the dwarves took her hands and gently pulled her back, away from the confrontation.

'Petra?' The huntsman was confused. 'Why won't you let her go home?'

'The spindle is broken.' Petra didn't take her eyes from the First Minister. 'He's going to kill her.'

'We don't have a choice,' the old man said. 'You know that. And so do these soldiers. Let me do this while she's still confused. For the sake of our kingdom. I will do it swiftly. She won't even know.'

The soldiers came closer, starting to encircle the huntsman and the small band with him, and he could see from their uniforms and the many weapons they carried, daggers, swords and knives sheathed from ankles to shoulders, that they were an elite unit, not normal soldiers who could be frightened away by the wolf or his blade, despite the creature's terrifying growl.

'This is not our fight, Petra,' the huntsman muttered. 'And perhaps he's right.' He remembered the serving girl he'd slept with the last time he'd met Beauty and her terrible fate. 'Perhaps she should die.'

'Maybe, but I can't carry that with me.' Petra pulled her knife and the stood firm. 'And I don't believe you could either.'

'Let me take her.' The First Minister came forward. 'Beauty. You must come with me. Your kingdom needs you.'

The dwarves had formed a tight circle around the queen, holding their tools as weapons, prepared to die defending a girl they didn't know, and the huntsman sighed.

'I'm afraid we can't allow that,' he said.

'Then you will all die too.'

The wolf snarled, but the huntsman caught a glint of silver in the moonlight further over to his right and realised there was a small team of archers hidden there, ready to take the wolf down as soon as he moved. Toby must have sensed them too as though he crouched, his bright fur rippling, he did not spring.

'Oh, I think you underestimate us.' Aladdin stepped forward, smiling at the old man. 'And I don't care who else dies here but I will peel your face from your skull with a spoon before I let you touch a hair on her head.' The huntsman looked across at him, surprised, and Aladdin shrugged. 'The other one is inside her. The one they want to kill. I *like* that one.'

'True love's kiss,' Petra said. 'Who'd have thought it possible?'

'Fate works in mysterious ways,' the huntsman added.

'What's happening?' Beauty pushed past the dwarves and came forward, upset and confused, and clasping the First Minister's hands. 'I don't understand. I keep forgetting things. And I woke up in an awful dungeon, and my head hurts and I'm frightened and I don't know why.'

As she spoke, clearly upset, the First Minister's hard expression evaporated. He loved the queen – *this* queen – and his shoulders slumped.

'I'm sorry,' he said. 'I'm so sorry.'

'He doesn't want you to leave,' Petra said. 'But we're just taking you to meet the prince's family before your wedding.' She looked at the First Minister. 'Let us take her. We'll look after her.' She smiled at Beauty. 'The prince is arranging a surprise for you in his kingdom.'

'And it'll be a surprise, that's for sure,' the huntsman said, thinking of the prince's new wife and Rumpelstiltskin and the baby and how Beauty would react to that. The Beast would make her presence felt, and Rose was clever, but not even she would be able to outwit that monster.

'Really?' Beauty's face lit up with joy and hope, and even though the huntsman knew her magic made them all want to protect her, he thought she really was the sweetest, most innocent girl and he could understand why they had resorted to a curse all those years ago, because it would be impossible to kill her any other way. He could see his own thoughts reflected on the First Minister's face.

'The Beast will come back,' he said. 'What will you do then?'

'That will be our problem, not yours.' Petra was resolute.

'What beast?' Beauty said, confused again, and Dreamy pulled her away, soothing her by showing her his pink silk scarf, telling her she could wear it as they travelled.

'If you let her return here . . .' the First Minister started, but the huntsman cut him off.

'We won't. You have my word.'

'Then we have a deal,' the First Minister said, and his relief was palpable. 'And you had better start your journey. Be as far away from here by morning as you can be. In case others decide to come after you.'

Eighteen

The following night they were sitting by the fireside, resting after a long night and day of travelling. They had stopped at Petra's grandmother's cottage for the two women to see each other for a brief, joyful moment, and to get more provisions, but they left Grouchy there with her, as it was clear that Aladdin and the Beast's was not the only true love to have been found on this adventure.

They travelled all day, until Toby transformed back into the wolf, and by the time the fire was dying down, the dwarves were already asleep. It was only then that Beauty spoke. She'd barely uttered a word throughout their journey and while Petra had tried to maintain the fantasy of going to the prince's kingdom, the huntsman realised that while Beauty was very sweet and believed the best in everyone, she wasn't stupid.

'Are you hungry?' he asked, holding out some of the rabbit they'd roasted, but she shook her head, hugging her knees to her chest.

'When I was a little girl,' she said softly, staring into the flickering flames that reflected back on her pale skin, dancing across it, 'I had a kitten called Domino. He was a present from Uncle Rumple for my fourth birthday. A little black and white thing with the softest fur. He followed me everywhere. I loved him so very, very much. I had him for three years and we were inseparable. He slept on my pillow even though my father disapproved. When I was seven, Domino went missing. He just vanished. It broke my heart. I couldn't believe he'd run away, and was sure something had happened to him, but he couldn't be found.'

She looked up from the fire, her eyes wells of sadness.

'Even then that didn't seem right to me. If something awful had happened to him, surely his body would have been found somewhere. But despite all the searches, Domino never came back. I cried for weeks, and then, as is the way of children – and perhaps in my nature – I began to smile and see the goodness in the world once more. No one spoke of Domino ever again.'

BLOOD

She paused and took a sip of dwarf beer, the small band of travellers silent as they listened, drawn into her story, even Aladdin was curious as Beauty spoke.

'I never told anyone – not Uncle Rumple, nor my beloved father, the king, or even Rapunzel, my best friend – that sometimes I dreamed of Domino. They weren't pleasant dreams. In my nightmares, I killed Domino with a pair of scissors and I was filled with a rage at him – a rage I didn't even know I was capable of. My hands were sticky with his blood and Uncle Rumple was staring at me, horrified, in the doorway. The dreams eventually faded, but others came instead. Equally terrible. More like jumbled half-memories than nightmares. I would push them out of my mind as soon as I woke as I couldn't bear to think of the things I was doing in them.'

She shivered where she sat, as if reliving the dreams, and learning anew what the Beast was capable of. The huntsman could only imagine the horror they filled the young woman, born to be the best of her people, with.

'And there have been times I don't remember at all. Whole nights and days that the First Minister and the others have brushed aside and told me I'm mistaken about, but that I *knew* were gone.' She looked at Petra and then Aladdin and finally the huntsman. 'The Beast you talk of is real, isn't she?'

The huntsman looked down at his boots, trying to find the best way to answer her without bringing the Beast back among them, his heart aching for her, but then she looked at Aladdin.

'You said you kissed the other one. Was she me too?'

'Her hair was different,' Aladdin said, matter-of-fact. 'It turned blonde where yours is black and vice versa. But really everything about her was different. She was – she is – I've never met anyone like her before. Like *me* before.'

'I killed Domino, didn't I?' Her voice was like glass breaking, and then her breath caught. 'And my father? Did I kill him too? Oh please, tell me I didn't.'

'You didn't.' It was Aladdin again. '*She* did. You said the bottle was vanilla flavouring. She knew it was poison.'

'So I did do it.' Tears sprung from her eyes with the horror of the realisation, and Petra immediately put her arm around the girl to soothe her.

'It's not your fault. You couldn't help it.'

'But she *is* me,' Beauty said. 'And they all hid it from me. Those dungeons . . . What have I done to my kingdom? My people?'

BLOOD

'They think she is your sister,' the huntsman said. She'd guessed enough of the truth now and she deserved to know the rest. 'When she awoke they called it a "dark day". They said she'd been allowed out from her place at the top of the castle. They did it all because they loved you.'

'The First Minister was right,' Beauty said, her shoulders straightening, and suddenly looking very much like a queen. 'I do have to die. But I won't ask you to do it. I will do it myself.' She looked at Aladdin. 'You have that poison I used to kill my father. I will use that.'

'No, you won't.' Aladdin was on his feet, angry now, immediately tossing the small bottle into the fire just as he'd burned the spindle. 'You're not her. You're nothing like her. What if you were *meant* to be two separate sisters? Have you considered that? You don't get to choose death for her.'

'She kills people,' the huntsman said. 'Hurts them.'

'She does what she was made to do,' Aladdin countered. 'I understand that. It's not easy being made differently from everyone else. And even if she does, then surely *this* pathetic sop of a girl shouldn't have to die because of the other one's deeds? Either way, it's not fair.'

'I hate to say it,' Petra said, stroking the large wolf's

head, who had laid itself on Beauty's lap, 'but I think he's right. There must be another way.'

'There is no other way,' Beauty said. 'And don't you see? I *want* to die. My poor father. How can I live knowing the things I've done?'

'What if we can separate them?' Aladdin said. 'I've lived a long time and I've seen the things magic can do. I've seen what it's done to *me*. There must be magic for this?' He looked around the group with more earnest passion than the huntsman had ever seen in the strange boy.

'Divide one soul into two?' Petra said. 'That's an unnatural magic.'

'But if it saves your precious Beauty, then what do you care?'

'And why do *you* care?' the huntsman asked. 'When the Beast will surely be put to death for her crimes anyway.'

Aladdin smiled, cold and calculated, and the huntsman could see how the Beast was his true love. 'Time will tell. And this at least buys her some time.'

'If you can separate us,' Beauty said, filled with a terrible hope. 'Then make me a child. An infant. Give the other one all our years. I cannot live with the memory of all this. I would rather be dead.'

'A baby?' The huntsman said, his skin tingling with the start of a plan. 'You'd want to be a baby?'

'Yes,' Beauty nodded, decisively. 'That's exactly what I want.'

Nineteen

The witch barely stirred after her long journey, her ankles sore from walking, but she was content to be with her family again. Sunk deep into the soft pillows and mattress, fresh crisp sheets and warm blankets heaped over her, she dreamed of a childhood long ago when her hair was golden, and she'd slept in rooms like these and all the world had been a glittering delight of life in the halo of royalty – so long ago, when she'd been a different person. When she'd been Rapunzel and not Gretel the witch. A dream of an old reality that felt more dream than real now.

As night hit its nadir in the early hours of the morning, the dream shifted and the fire returned.

She was running through the castle as it burned

white-hot around her, the hem of her dress aflame, and everything was so bright and hot she could barely breathe. She was so lost in the visions that the noise of the people arriving into the courtyard below barely registered as she tossed and turned, sweating in her sleep.

When she woke with a start, there was bright daylight outside and her sweat had cooled, and her mind was clear, and her beloved great-granddaughter Lilith the ice queen was sitting on the side of her bed, holding a breakfast tray.

'A pot of nettle tea,' she said, placing it on the bedside table, before putting a full plate on the witch's knee as she sat up in bed. 'And fresh bread and the finest honey with butter just churned and a few pastries to follow. All your favourites.'

'You're a good girl,' the witch said, ravenously hungry and knowing that there was no honey as sweet as that from royal hives. 'Now tell me what happened while I slept.'

She listened as Lilith told her about the huntsman and the dwarves' return, and the unhappy young queen now locked in a fine suite of rooms but under vigilant guard, and the idea they'd had that might solve all their problems.

'Quite something,' the witch said, flaky crumbs

dropping onto the bedclothes as she chewed the last pastry, thoughtful.

'It was the genie's idea. He's not to be trusted, but he's clever.'

'You have a genie?'

'I don't use the wishes, don't worry.'

The witch ruminated on the information. 'It *is* possible. But the magic required . . .' Her head throbbed just thinking about it. 'Well, it would have to be fierce. Dangerous. We'll need witch's blood. Mine and yours and hers, if she's from water witch stock.'

'One drop for the gentlest touch, two for strong magic, but three is always too much?' Lilith said.

The old witch knew only too well the power of three drops or more. 'It *will* be more than three. It will be painful.' She looked up at Lilith, excited by the challenge. 'But perhaps it's time to prove we've earned our own witch's blood.'

'The fire you've dreamed of,' Lilith said. 'Dragon song?'

The old woman nodded.

'I did some research in some of mother's books I'd hidden in the library. They say a dragon comes at a pure witch's birth. And a pure witch can summon one – only once.'

The old witch didn't need her great-granddaughter

to tell her. She'd passed those books to her daughter and then her granddaughter, Lilith's mother.

'A pure witch can summon a dragon for once in a lifetime magic. Once in a generation. For magic that is fated.' She sipped her nettle tea. 'And therein lies the first risk. Everyone always believes their need is fated. Not every need is. And that is if I'm a pure witch at all, and I have doubts about that.'

'You've lived as long as one,' Lilith said. 'You've outlived my mother and grandmother. You will probably outlive me. That's the way of pureblood witches. You must be one.'

'Someone will have to ride the dragon if we summon it.' This was not the time to explain to Lilith how she came to become a witch and why she hesitated to claim to be pureblood. She had no doubt that Gretel had been, and she'd been Gretel for such a long time that witchcraft was second nature to her, but perhaps it was indeed a second nature. Still, there was only one way to find out. And she had to trust her dreams and the willingness of all these people to do something to save the young queen Beauty from herself. 'To make sure it sings in the right place,' she continued. 'Someone brave and kind and true. And there will be a risk. Dragons cannot be tamed, and it has been a long time since one has been summoned.

They might kill the rider. They might kill us all.'

'But shall we try?' Lilith asked, and the old witch smiled, her eyes twinkling.

'Oh, of course we shall, my dear. It will be fun. But we must prepare. First, we will need a raven. And then we shall collect the blood.'

***

There were two days left before Rumpelstiltskin's deadline when the raven arrived, a glittering red jewel in the feathers of its neck declaring it an emissary from the Queens of the Kingdom of Plenty and containing the tightly wound scroll that once again gave Rose hope to cling to. She had tried to stay strong for her husband but as the days had passed, and with no word coming from the huntsman or the dwarves, even Rose had lain awake at night, her stomach in knots, starting to fear that they were going to lose their beautiful Giselle, their world, and that their hearts would never recover.

She read the message three times, her heart leaping with possibility, before sharing it with her beloved prince, who burst into tears, their precious Giselle gurgling happily between them. Once she had calmed both herself and him down, she sent a message to

Rumpelstiltskin – who they'd found rooms for in the castle despite every part of her wanting to put as much space between her child and the man who wanted to claim her – and when he'd arrived they were every inch the royal couple, contained and polite and calm, as she put the prospect of a *different* baby to him.

'No!' he exclaimed, pacing the room, his lined face contorted with anger. 'I told you, I will accept no other baby than a royal baby. Your child is mine and in two days I will take her.'

'What about Beauty?'

'What do you mean?' His feet stopped and his eyes narrowed. 'Beauty is a young woman, not a baby. And we know she can never be allowed to live.'

'But if she were a baby again, cured of her second personality, would you want her? Instead of my child?'

'It's not possible.' His face was defiant but there was a shred of hope in his eyes. He'd loved Beauty, Rose knew that. He could love her again. 'Beauty cured and alive? I would have to see it with my own eyes to know it is not trickery. And you must bring Giselle. The clock is ticking.'

'Of course.' Rose got to her feet. Her heart was racing with nerves but she did not let her fear show. 'There is no time to waste. We must reach the Kingdom of Plenty by tomorrow night. We will take a guard and travel immediately.'

'I should stay here,' the prince said quietly, his face awash with shame. 'If Beauty sees me. It might . . .' He hesitated, looking for the least hurtful words. 'I don't want my presence to cause any problems.'

Rose understood. For them it was just over two years since he had encountered Beauty and the Beast, but no doubt the young queen still thought of him as her beloved. What would seeing him again do to her? Would it bring the Beast back out? Aside from all that, Rose wouldn't want to put him in that position. He was a different man now and the past was the past.

'Tell your father I've taken Giselle and gone to visit Cinderella in the woods. He won't question that.' She kissed him, and although this problem was of his making, she felt a rush of love for him. 'We will be back soon. Don't worry.'

'I love you, Rose,' he whispered. 'More than I ever dreamed I could love a woman.' They held each other tightly and she almost couldn't let him go.

'It will all be fine.' She forced a smile. 'You'll see.'

'I know it will.' He smiled back, equally forced. 'Because you are my clever, brilliant Rose and you can solve anything.'

BLOOD

She knew the thought gave him comfort but she also knew this was out of her hands. Whether this could be done or not all came down to magic, and that was not one of her skills.

***

Giselle slept in the papoose at Rose's chest for most of the journey, waking only for feeding or to point at things in the forest and make excited baby noises and chatter, and Rose did not speak to Rumpelstiltskin until the Kingdom of Plenty came into view. There was no point in trying to change his mind and she wanted to have this time with her child. He respected that and rode ahead with two soldiers, while the other four brought up the rear. When the spires of the castle cut into the horizon, the Far Mountain beyond as it always was wherever you were in the kingdoms, Rose finally let her horse catch up with his.

'Before we face whatever will come, I must say this.' At her chest, Giselle played with loose strands of her mother's dyed red hair, unaware that her fate was being decided. 'My husband has many flaws, and it is hard to forgive him for what he promised you, but he is a good father. And he is becoming a good husband and will be a good king.'

'People change,' Rumpelstiltskin said, staring towards the castle and avoiding her gaze.

'Yes, they do. You were once a good and noble man. I can see the embers of it in you, but now you are filled with bitterness. My husband did not take your daughter. And if this plan fails and you take my child, you will be as bad as the witch who tricked you into giving up Rapunzel. But I hope, if the worst comes to pass, that Giselle will make you a better man. Even though you will never be able to tell her the truth without her hating you for it. That will be the burden you will have to bear.'

She saw that her words hit their mark like a sharp arrow as Rumpelstiltskin flinched, and she moved her horse forward. It was the truth and he needed to consider it.

But, as they headed into the magic-kissed kingdom, late afternoon shifting to evening, she hoped beyond hope that the huntsman's plan would work.

Twenty

It was dark by the time they reached the clearing in the forest, a vast circle off the beaten track, hidden by the dense foliage. A place where moss no longer grew and the old trees bore scorch marks from stories long ago forgotten, of a time when the dragons were awake and lived side by side amongst the people of the Far Mountain.

Lilith knew the stories told that the dragons vanished because they simply wanted to sleep, and their night could be several centuries long, but knowing people as she did, and knowing the cruelty she herself had once been capable of, she wondered what men had done to drive them back to the Far Mountain and force their long sleep upon them. It was said they woke and flew and lived among the giants beyond the mountain, but the giants were probably simply stories to frighten children and no one had ever been to the other side to prove them true or otherwise. The Far Mountain was like an illusion. It was everywhere and nowhere. To find the steep cliff face took a seasoned guide, and even then a traveller could end up walking in circles and never getting any closer. No one in her lifetime had ever scaled it, no matter what drunk wanderers claimed in taverns.

But this, she thought, as they walked to the centre of the scorched earth, had been a dragon landing at some point, that much was obvious. Her heart fluttered with worry, even as Snow strode confidently ahead. She was unafraid, as ever, and her bravery made Lilith worry more. But Snow had wanted an adventure, and she wanted to do this, and Lilith could not stop her and would never try. Either way, the hour was nearly upon them, and there was no turning back now.

'This will do. If we can summon a dragon anywhere, this will be the place.' Lilith's great-grandmother came to a halt, and pushed back the hood of her cape, and nodded, satisfied. Rose and Rumpelstiltskin had arrived not long before they themselves headed into the woods, but the old woman hadn't wanted to see them. *This is not the time,* she'd said, and Lilith hadn't pushed her, even though she found it strange.

She'd thought her great-grandmother would want to get the measure of Rose and the bitter man before they all took this risk for them, but it seemed not. They would be fine with the huntsman, Toby and Petra, and the dwarves would do their best to keep everyone's spirits up. Aladdin was back in his lamp for now, but she had promised she'd release him to speak to the Beast after it was all said and done, and she'd keep the lamp with her when the magic took place. There was a good chance they would all burn to death anyway, and if that was happening, she'd decided it might as well happen to him, too.

In the pale light of the moon, Snow's eyes were alight with energy and excitement, her pink cheeks flushed against her pale skin. Lilith thought she'd never looked so beautiful. The air around them was close, and although it was relatively early the city streets had been quiet as their horses had clopped through them, as if the promise of magic had sent them subconsciously to the safety of their houses and beds.

'Are you sure you want to do this?' she asked Snow for the hundredth time, and her wife and lover smiled.

'More than anything. And you know as well as I do

141

that I'm the only person who has a hope of being *able* to do it.'

Lilith knew she was right. Stallions broke for Snow White as soon as she stroked their flanks, and her goodness was a light in the darkest ocean. The fairest in the land and beyond, that was her Aurelia.

'Then I wish you luck. Be safe, my love.' She leaned in and kissed Snow's cherry red lips, savouring the sweetness of them, committing it to memory despite assuring herself that all would be well.

The old witch came forward and opened the vial of thick blood, a mixture of her own, Lilith's and Beauty's, drawn but an hour before, the magic in it still keeping it warm. Snow held out her hands and the witch smeared the palms until they were dark as the night, and then drew a line across her forehead and nose like warpaint.

'Remember,' the old woman said. 'You only need to feel. Don't try to tell the creature what to do. Think about what is right. What is good. Share what you want from it through your feelings. It will decide for itself. You have to surrender to it. Do you understand? Even though it might kill you.'

'Yes.' Snow smiled softly. 'Just like love.'

The witch closed her eyes and held Snow's face in her wrinkled hands, muttering words Lilith couldn't hear and wouldn't understand if she did, an older magic than she had studied, a magic that ran to the bone, and as her whispers melted into the air, the wind picked up, suddenly strong, moaning through the trees as it carried the spell far away to where it needed to be heard, whipping branches sideways with its power, although in the circle there wasn't so much as a breeze.

When her great-grandmother had finished and stillness ruled the forest once more, Lilith watched the old woman's shoulders slump forward and saw that the redness of her cheery complexion had faded to a powdery white almost as pale as her hair. Her full cheeks had sunk a little into her bones and her body was trembling. Magic was never really a gift, Lilith thought. There was always something to pay for it. She could see her great-grandmother was already exhausted, and they had barely begun. Still, the expression in her eyes was strong and she straightened back up. Something was different about her since Rose and Rumpelstiltskin had arrived, but Lilith wasn't sure what.

'One is waking.' The old witch turned to look towards the Far Mountain, its dark, familiar shape always visible against the backdrop of the night. 'It will come. And when the moon is directly over that ash tree, that is when we must be ready.'

'How will I know if it will let me ride it?' Snow asked.

'Because, my dear,' Lilith's great-grandmother replied, matter-of-fact, 'you will still be alive.'

***

Beauty was as sweet-natured as he remembered her, so it broke Rumpelstiltskin's heart to see the deep sorrow she felt now. She had run to him and hugged him hard and they had both cried quietly for their shame and their parts in each other's tragedies, and now, as the moon rose high in the night's sky, they sat side by side on the bed in the room she'd been given to wait in, studying each other in the candlelight.

'I'm sorry if I seem a little confused.' Beauty took his hand, like she did when she was a little girl. 'I asked them to give me a potion. To make sure I stay calm. In case *she* decides to change our minds about this. It's so strange. Now that I know about her, I realise she's always been there, trying to get out. I can feel her. I think she wants us to be separated as much as I do.'

Her eyes were bleary, not only from her tears, but from whatever Lilith had given her, and she yawned some more, leaning her head on his bony shoulder.

'For me, it's only been a few days since I last saw you. For you, so much has happened.'

'Do you understand how dangerous this is?' he asked, pulling her close. 'It could kill you.'

'If we can't be separated then I would rather die.' Her voice was soft. 'You were right to curse me. I did terrible things. My own father.' Her tears fell again, and he could see that this magic was truly her only chance. To be wiped free of it. To start again. He stroked her glossy black hair, and then, in a moment of forgiveness, stroked the blonde streaks too.

'You were not responsible. And despite it all, I am glad that the spindle didn't work.'

'You have suffered so much for me, Uncle Rumple. Poor Rapunzel, now long gone. You loved her so. I loved her so. How can you ever forgive me?'

There were tears in his eyes when he squeezed her hand tightly. 'You were always like a second daughter to me, Beauty. And if this works, I would like to be a father to you. If you will allow it.'

'I would like that very much,' she replied and hugged him tightly. 'I love you, Uncle Rumple.'

He hugged her back, for as long as he could, knowing that he was hugging the Beast too, and that in this moment they all needed comfort, for who knew if any of them would survive the night.

It was only when the low tolling of a quiet bell summoned them that they broke free.

'I'm ready,' she said, and kissed him on the cheek as the door to her rooms unlocked and Dreamy and Feisty emerged to escort them. 'We're both ready.'

Twenty-One

Snow White *felt*, more than saw, the dragon arriving.

She'd been waiting, with a mixture of nerves and excitement, time passing so slowly, wondering if the magic hadn't worked and so eager to get started, but then, as the sky darkened and the temperature around her dropped and then rose, almost simultaneously, she felt the first flush of fear. Her eyes began to ache, the air above the forest shimmering pearlescent, and her ears rang loud from the shift in pressure. Around her, as the small forest animals fled into burrows, birds took to the skies, attempting to flee from the monster that approached. They did not fly far, instead falling like heavy rain, dropping to the clearing floor and into the canopy of the trees, stunned unconscious by the energy that filled the sky as the dragon roared, creating a thunder that shook the forest.

Something terrible was coming. Something terrible and wonderful and so far beyond her understanding, Snow White was suddenly filled with so much horror, she almost called out that it was all a mistake and she couldn't do it, and the dragon was going to kill her. The dragon was going to kill all of them for their arrogance.

It was coming towards her and it was coming fast. She couldn't see it, other than shimmering edges in air, but she could hear the heavy beat of wings and felt the heat of its breath as it swooped down from overhead. It was going to destroy her, she was sure of it, and she ducked, covering her head with her arms, and squeezed her eyes shut, as the dragon skimmed the top of the clearing before heading upwards to circle once again in the skies, the disdain in its alien roar threatening to burst her eardrums, before again, diving down to the clearing, a hurricane of wind in its wake.

Snow White, curled up on the forest floor, focused on the darkness behind her eyes, shutting all else out. She swallowed her fear down, and centred herself. She would not die here, paralysed by fear. At the very least she would face the dragon, she would stand her ground as she did with the stallions and the mares, and if she was to die, it would be with love for the creature in her heart, for they were the ones who had dragged it here, and it was only doing as all creatures did – obeying its nature.

With every ounce of her strength, she pulled herself to her feet, and stood tall, tilting her face skywards. This time when the dragon swooped down over her she did not move, but stood firm and raised one hand up, reaching out to touch it even if she couldn't see it. She would not be afraid. She was not afraid.

She felt it then, hot scaly skin against her palm, ridges old as the rock of the Far Mountain itself. She gasped and smiled, and then it was gone again, up high above. For a moment, the air was still again, and then once more came the heavy beat of the wings, but this time the wind was calmer and cooler, and the earth shuddered as the great beast landed.

Snow White didn't move and could barely breathe, but then she felt the creature shift from foot to foot in front of her, and then suddenly, it showed itself, the scaly body taking up half the clearing and it was at least three times Snow White's height. The dragon was magnificent. It shone and glittered, bright as the finest gold from the Eastern Seas, and shimmering with heat. Its eyes flashed green and red and cobalt blue like the finest jewels dug out from the earth by the hardy dwarves, and they swirled in circles as if all of the kingdoms existed in them and more.

Snow knew in that moment that if she were to die that night, then it was worth it to have seen and known a dragon. She stepped forward, reaching out with both hands tentatively exploring the creature. Its muzzle was wide, with a high gnarled ridge running through the middle, and flared nostrils on each side, and her fingers moved downwards, touching the teeth as wide as her fist and smooth and hard as marble.

'Hello,' she whispered, finding she was silently crying with the enormity of it all. 'It's an honour to meet you.'

As her hands stroked the rough skin, she leaned forward, as she would with her stallion, and rested her head against the dragon's scaly neck. It snorted slightly then, a sound that made the ground reverberate beneath them, but Snow White didn't flinch, pressing her body against the creature and soothing it with her calmness. Her palms were on its muzzle still when she felt a hot wetness that made her gasp, like almost-burning honey sticking to skin, and she realised the dragon was licking her – tasting the blood on her palms.

It shuddered, and so did she, and then it was there

– the connection she'd been told to expect, the dragon reaching into her mind, evaluating her.

The forest was forgotten, and as her head spun with the dizzying enormity of it, she became a tiny inconsequential speck in the cavern of the ancient creature's mind, filled with centuries and centuries of life and memory and love and terror and things she knew she could never understand. She also knew that if she allowed herself to fully *see* it, she'd be lost in there – driven mad – for ever.

She made herself even smaller and remembered what Lilith's great-grandmother had said. With her head there, against the dragon's, she thought of the tragedy of Beauty, of everything that had befallen her and her kingdom, of all of those who'd suffered, and she let the dragon learn it through her, through her empathy and emotions, the loss, the fear, the bravery and the love of all involved.

When the dragon pulled away, severing the connection, she fell to the forest floor, sweating and close to broken herself. She had never been as *known*, not even by Lilith, as she was now known by the dragon.

'Will you help me?' she asked, her mouth dry, as she sank to her knees.

The dragon dipped its head, and crouched, and she carefully climbed onto its back, sitting between two of the spikes in the ridge that ran from its head to the tip of its tail. She hooked her feet under the edges of its wings, and held on tight.

She didn't need to tell the dragon where to go. It knew her and her thoughts and her hopes, and as it lifted up into the air, the gold fading once more to a shimmering invisibility and this time doing the same to Snow, despite the seriousness of the task ahead, she could not help but laugh with the joy of it.

Twenty-Two

Petra's stomach was in knots as she stood at the window, looking down on the sleeping city, torches dotted here and there, keeping them safe. How safe were they? If this went wrong would the whole city burn? Would she ever see her grandmother again? Did they have the right to even attempt this? Was this Beauty's magic at work on them?

'I can see you thinking.' Toby slid his arms around her waist and kissed her neck. 'But the time for that is over. Listen.'

Above them the second set of bells rang quietly, the signal that everything was ready and they should come to the terrace at the highest point of the castle, in the centre of the turret.

'We should go.' Behind them, the huntsman drained

his wine. Petra took a deep breath, and she and Toby followed him to the stairs. Toby was right. There was no time to change their minds, and so she pushed her fear down deep inside her. She knew in her heart that this was the right thing to do, and if it went wrong, she hoped they would be the only ones who suffered the consequences. She had lived well and felt true love. She was lucky.

They climbed the narrow spiral stairs, up and up, only the sound of her heartbeat, their breathing and their footsteps for company, until finally they reached the top. The huntsman pushed the heavy wooden door open and as she stepped out onto the surprisingly large stone terrace, and saw that they were nearly in the clouds, she shivered. They were so high the very air was colder and thinner and she felt a world away from the sleeping citizens below.

As they made their way to join the dwarves and Lilith at a far wall, she realised no one had taken up the witch's offer of staying inside or leaving the castle for their own safety. They could not leave, she real- ised – they were all a part of this adventure, and the witch had said that the magic would need them all to will it well, and it seemed that the general consensus was that if everything went wrong then they may as well burn in the fresh air rather than hiding in their rooms. Lilith's ice-white hair lifted in the breeze and Petra thought she'd never looked so beautiful, her face turned to the sky, searching with longing, the bronze lamp in one clenched fist.

'She'll be all right,' Petra said, taking her free hand and squeezing it.

'I know,' Lilith said, keeping hold of her. 'If she wasn't, we'd see the forest burning by now.'

As they held each other's hands, the need for contact unspoken, Petra thought it was a strange sight to be faced with, more like something from the Beast's balls than a magic coming from goodness. The young queen, Beauty, stood in the centre of the terrace, blood smeared on her face and hands and dress – witch's blood – and Rumpelstiltskin was perhaps ten feet away, as close as he was allowed. The old witch, Gretel, wore a hooded robe, her face obscured, perhaps fifteen feet from Beauty, facing her, and drops of blood, left like a dark trail of pebbles on the sand-coloured flagstones, connected the two.

As the old woman held her hands up, blood on her palms as well, and started to chant, Petra's breath caught in her chest. The wind was picking up. And there was something, almost a light in the darkness, a shape that shimmered pearlescent but couldn't be seen, first in the distance, but as the witch's chanting grew louder, it began to fill her vision.

When her ears pounded with the sound of great beating wings, her heart racing in fear, the small group huddled tighter together, and Lilith whispered, *'It's here.'*

And then all they could do was wait for the dragon to sing.

***

Snow White was no longer sure where she ended and the dragon began.

As they soared towards the castle, the terrace visible far below them, she realised it was perhaps the most wonderful feeling – other than Lilith's love – that she had ever experienced.

On the terrace far below she could see her beloved Lilith looking up, her brave dwarves and the other adventurers beside her, the witch with her hands held high, calling them forth, letting the blood draw the dragon.

But Beauty was at the centre of it all, a tiny, fragile figure so filled with potent energy. Snow could see what the dragon saw, the fight between two people for one body, the magic of their creation, a person who should never have been.

BLOOD

As they swept down closer, power thrummed through every beat of wings and the air tightened around them, drawing in, preparing for the magnitude of what was to come.

And then it happened.

The dragon started to sing.

Its white fire – bursting free from wide jaws, vibrating through its body, creating the soft high note of celestial music to accompany its terrible heat – rained down on Beauty, targeting only her but filling the sky with brightness. At first, Snow White felt a rush of joy at the purity of it, and then, as the dragon trembled beneath her, she realised something was wrong. She felt it from the dragon as Beauty screamed below them, twisting and turning – falling, writhing, to the floor – she *heard* it from the dragon, a message without words, as if she and it were one.

The dragon dived lower and as they almost skimmed the heads of those below, Snow White screamed, as loudly as she could, 'More blood! You need stronger blood!'

Twenty-Three

The air roared with heat as the dragon sang again, the jet of white flame engulfing the girl in front of her, but as the seconds passed all the witch could hear was Beauty's screams of agony. In turn she was engulfed by her own panic. What had she done? Her blood *wasn't* good enough. Even after all these years she wasn't truly the witch, but as much a mismatch of body and nature as the burning queen in front of her, and suddenly she felt like a child again. As she cried out in shame and horror, she wished she could throw her hood off and run to Rumpelstiltskin, her father, to make it all better as he had when she was small.

'More blood!' Snow White had called from above. 'You need stronger blood!' and the witch knew they were all doomed. She was burning poor Beauty for nothing, as if she was the cruel King of the Winter Lands herself. She called out for the burning to end, praying for the death to be quicker, but as Beauty's screams grew louder, she knew the dragon's song was keeping her in limbo, threatening to keep her on fire for ever. She was about to run to the young queen and drag them both over the side of the terrace to fall to a merciful death, when through the brightness she saw Rumpelstiltskin running forward, towards the burning queen.

'I have it!' he cried out suddenly, tugging a small vial from inside his jacket pocket. 'I have more blood!'

Her breath almost stopped, the clock rewinding so fast in her memory. She knew that bottle. How could she forget it? It was the vial of Aunt Gretel's blood. She'd put two drops on Conrad's blanket, and then Aladdin had used it to switch Aunt Gretel and her permanently.

Blood which had come from this body when someone else lived in it. When body and soul had combined to create a pure witch. That was Gretel's blood.

'No!' she called out as she realised what Rumpelstiltskin, her beloved father so long forgotten, was about to do, but her shout was too late to stop him and she knew that nothing would. Her joy turned to terror as she watched Rumpelstiltskin running into the blaze with it, reaching for the burning girl, tilting the vial as he went.

She screamed, and started to run towards him, but then the dragon sang again, and everything was fire and brightness and the world trembled as she fell to her knees, sure her eardrums would burst from the sound, and her heart broke for the father she was losing once again.

Her ears were ringing for so long, her face pressed to the ground, her arms over her head, that it was only when she heard a woman laughing that she realised the world was still once again and the dragon had gone. Slowly, she looked up, full of dread, and gasped at what she saw. First her eyes widened as she smiled, then tears of joy sprang to her eyes.

The terrible fire had gone and they were once more in the cool, night air, lit only by torches, but as she pulled her old and aching body from the ground, the witch could see that everything had changed.

Her father was not dead, but stood, untouched by the flames, holding a black-haired infant of maybe a year or eighteen months, in his arms. Beside him stood a beautiful blonde, the laughing woman, who was studying herself.

'You're the Beast,' Petra said, coming forward, curious.

'Not very polite,' the woman purred, her eyes sharp, amused and dangerous, like a cat around a mouse. 'They called *her* Beauty. Well, from now on I shall be Belle.' She tilted her head. 'No, actually, Bella. Like Belladonna. I think that would be apt.' She spun around and laughed again. 'I'm me. But I feel lighter. As if I can walk on air.'

'That's because you have no magic left in your bones.' The witch came forward, her own limbs like lead. 'It's gone. The song has taken it.'

'Where's Snow?' Lilith looked skywards, worried. 'Why isn't she here?'

'She'll be back,' the witch reassured her. 'Don't worry.'

Nervous, she turned her attention to Rumpelstiltskin, her heart racing in her chest. Her beloved father. He'd never abandoned her. He'd never stopped loving her. Even if his love had made him so bitter he could no longer see right from wrong. But then, there had been many years in the forest when she had taken her desire for revenge on Aladdin out on rude and spoiled children who found her cottage in the woods. Wickedness was not wholly owned by the wicked. She slowly pulled her hood down, revealing her white hair and ruddy face above her stocky body.

'You!' His eyes blazed with rage, and she could see

he was only restrained by holding the infant Beauty in his arms, or he would attack her. 'How can it be you? I should kill you for what you did!'

'It's *me*, father.' The tears came fast and thick, more tears than she'd shed in the hundred years since she sobbed for him in that room in Gretel's tower, sobbed so hard that the witch used magic to take her pain away. '*Rapunzel*. It's me.'

'Don't you dare.' He backed away, the pain of his loss fresh in his face. 'You are a trickster and a fiend.'

'Your jacket.' She stepped forward, reaching for the sleeve. 'You tore the cuff on a stable gate and I mended it as a surprise overnight. The First Minister wanted you to get the tailor to make you a new one fit for your standing but you told him that I had taken an ordinary jacket and made it perfect with my efforts.' She wiped her nose with the back of her veined hand and half-laughed. 'Even though it was clear my stitching wasn't good and I pricked my finger about five times while doing it.'

'It can't be.' He stared at her, his skin deathly pale. The others had gathered round, drawn into the story, even Bella curious.

'I met a young king. He was a foolish man, but I was a foolish girl and I thought I loved him. I wanted to test him. So Aunt Gretel – and you must know she loved me and she regretted what she did – she and I used a glimmer spell to look like each other. But *that boy* secretly added more blood and I became her and she became me.'

He came closer and she put her old hand on his old face and smiled. 'It's me, Father, it really is. The witch, Gretel, married Conrad and stayed in the village and had a daughter. She kept my name and I kept hers. We both had daughters.' She glanced back at Lilith. 'And Lilith is my great-granddaughter. *Your* great-great granddaughter.'

'So the woman I thought was my great-grandmother was actually Gretel the witch?' Petra took the infant from Rumpelstiltskin's arms. 'Not Rapunzel – you – at all.'

'She was Gretel, but no longer the witch. Her body held her magic and I was in her body. And she was a pure witch. One in a hundred perhaps. That's why I have lived so long.'

Rumpelstiltskin came closer to her, staring into her eyes. 'I felt no connection with the old lady in the woods, kind and sweet as she was. But she said her mother would stare at the forest wall, upset. Why would she do that if she was not my child?'

'Guilt,' the witch answered. 'She knew what she'd done was wrong. She knew you were suffering.

163

I suppose she hoped to speak to you, but couldn't find the words.'

'My child,' he finally gasped, and pulled her to him and the witch felt young again as they laughed and cried and laughed some more.

'I hated Aladdin for so long for what he did to me,' she said eventually when they broke apart. 'But it was worth it for this.'

'Aladdin?' Lilith stared at her, confused. 'How do you know Aladdin?'

The witch looked back, now confused herself. Surely the boy was long dead by now. 'How do *you* know Aladdin?'

'Well,' Bella spoke for them all, her smile showing off her sharp white teeth, as her equally sharp eyes danced around the group. 'Now, this *is* getting interesting.'

Twenty-Four

'I can explain.' Aladdin rarely felt nervous, but seeing the sparks crackling at the witch's fingertips, his mouth dried. He was good at thinking on his feet but it had only been moments since Lilith summoned him from the lamp and now he was face-to-face with Rapunzel in Gretel's body, and she clearly wasn't as happy as he was about their reunion.

They were in a hexagonal reception room he hadn't seen before, high up in the tower, and he looked around the group hoping for some support, and perhaps even a sip of the warm red wine they were drinking. Neither was forthcoming. He knew the huntsman thought he was dangerous, and Petra and Toby, side by side, didn't even smile. The dwarves were eating their fill of the bread and cheese and cold meats laid out and were paying him no attention at all.

'I don't understand what you're so upset about,' he continued. 'I only wanted what was best for you.'

'How was this the best for me?' the witch said, incredulous. 'Or for her?'

'Oh Rapunzel, you're forgetting what it was like,' he pleaded, hoping he sounded reasonable. He was being honest after all. 'What you thought you wanted? I had to save you from it! Marrying some rich fool more in love with himself than with you? You'd only have realised what a falsehood it would become when it was too late. You'd have been bored. I wanted you to have a more interesting life. I *liked* you. Before I met Bella you were the only person I'd ever really liked. Everyone else is so tedious. You were fun. So yes, I changed you with the witch, and now she's long dead and here you are reunited with your father. She was happy in her simple life, and you've been happy in yours.' He waved his hands through the air in frustration. 'So maybe, yes, I went about it the wrong way. But I'm not like other people. I don't think like them and I don't *feel* like them. I did my best.' He paused, and shrugged, helpless. 'Most of the people I meet have far bloodier ends. I *thought* I was giving you a gift.'

BLOOD

Although he kept his eyes on the witch, he felt Bella, his beautiful Beast, inching closer, and he knew that she, like he had, would be taking inventory of anything in the room, from a candlestick to the fire poker to a breakable wine glass or bottle that could be used as a weapon, should it come to that. They might not win, but they would go down fighting and covered in blood, together.

'You *are* happy. Tell me I'm wrong about that,' he finished.

The crackling at the witch's fingertips faded away and she met his gaze. 'No, you are not wrong,' she said finally. 'I have had a long life and while I have lost some of those I love I have my Lilith and Snow, and now my father back. We have a second chance to be a family again.' She took the gurgling infant from Rumpelstiltskin and sat her on her ample hip. 'I will help him raise Beauty to be the queen her kingdom deserves and our three kingdoms have forged a unbreakable alliance.' She looked at Rose and Lilith, who nodded in agreement, smiling.

'So, there you go,' Aladdin said. 'Maybe I did a good thing.' This was as good a chance as any to try his luck. He smiled as obsequiously as he could manage at the keeper of his lamp. 'And so perhaps you could set me free?'

'Are you mad?' Lilith stared at him. 'I told you I'd *never* set you free. You do too much harm. You murder on a whim. I offered you the deal for your help and I will stand by it. Two weeks out of the lamp once a year, with no harm to anyone.'

His blood froze in his veins. The smell of the tarnished metal. The sense of being trapped. Buried alive. The endless tedium. He couldn't live like that in exchange for two weeks of curtailed freedoms. It was his breaking point. 'I cannot live in that metal prison for ever.' He looked at Rose and he was deadly serious. 'I have heard of the Troll Road in your kingdom. Throw me from that.'

'I doubt you have any intention of letting me live long, either,' a seductively smooth voice said as a soft hand took his, holding it tight. Bella. 'So throw us together.' She leaned in to him, purring in his ear. 'We'd take the troll with us at the very least.'

'Perhaps that would be for the best,' Lilith said slowly. 'Both of you have an unnatural cruelty. You have committed terrible crimes. Under any rule of law you would both be condemned to death. If the Troll Road is your choice, then so be it.'

'*Wait.*'

The voice was so unexpected that even Aladdin startled, before turning with the others to see Snow, standing on the ledge of the window, her face shining with joy. Beyond, as night turned to day, the dragon's golden scales refracted the dawn's sunlight creating a glittering rainbow around itself as the air warmed with its gentle breath.

Snow jumped down into the room and took an apple from the table, holding it out through the window, rubbing the dragon's nose as it ate.

'Aladdin and the girl can't change. They are who they are,' Snow said. 'And there has been enough wickedness already. While they may have blood on their hands, I do not want theirs on ours.'

'What do you suggest?' Lilith asked her. 'If you have a solution, I would gladly hear it.'

'They *both* go into the lamp.' Snow picked up a glass of wine and drained it in one. 'And you seal it up.'

'I thought you said no cruelty?' Aladdin snarled. 'And you can't do that to Bella. She doesn't know how tedious it is in there! A plain room with a sandy floor and the stench of metal for all eternity without even a glimpse of sunlight? It will drive us both mad.'

'But what if there could be more to it than that?' Beauty looked to Lilith and then to the witch. 'I was listening from outside. How powerful a glimmer can you create? Can you fill the lamp with an illusion? A world of their own to explore? All of the kingdoms.

The seas. The people. None of it real, but real for them?'

Was such a thing possible? Aladdin's heart leapt. It would be freedom. And as for only being the illusion of it, well, he'd never considered other people truly real at all anyway.

'Now that is a thought,' Gretel murmured, her shoulders straightening. 'Make it bigger on the inside? There must be some magic for that.'

'Really?' Lilith said. 'You would gift them this life?'

'Yes,' the witch said thoughtfully. 'As I suppose he did gift me mine.'

'And after all,' Snow White said, as she took Lilith's hand, and kissed her long and hard and warm. 'Every true love deserves a happy ending.'

***

All was well that ended well.

The sun shone down brightly, warm in May, and Lilith and Snow waved at the cheering crowds below who were happy that their queens had returned from their visit to the Kingdom of Light and Glass. Lilith was happy too. It had been wonderful to see her great-grandmother and Rumpelstiltskin, and share their joy in being reunited, and the baby Beauty was growing up to be everything good in the world.

The emotional scars her great-grandmother and her father had carried for so many years were gone and everyone could see they doted on the child they were raising between them. After living for so long with so many secrets, they had taken the brave decision to be honest with Beauty's people, and when the truth had been shared, it was clear how much the city loved Beauty, because they rallied around and swore to protect their infant queen. They had become a truly happy family in another contented kingdom, and it was wonderful that Lilith and Snow White could be part of that. The kingdoms seemed settled after so much adventure, and the discovery of the lost tenth land. The prince and Rose had beautiful Giselle, the huntsman and Cinderella were both back in their beloved forests, and now that her grandmother and Grouchy were content, Petra and Toby were considering a move south, to the warmth and the olive trees of Nature's Keep.

It was wonderful that they had all these family and friends to visit when they wanted but their own hearts belonged here at home, where the cherry blossom bloomed bright, ravens cawed, and the air was often disturbed by the beat of a golden dragon's wings. Beside her Snow laughed merrily as the dragon, much like them all now, no longer afraid to show her colours, ducked and dove across the sky, full of energy and excitement that they were back.

The dragon had never left after it sang for them. Like all the creatures of the kingdoms, it had fallen in love with Snow White's kindness, and had made its home in the highest tower of the castle, and the dwarves had dug out the hardiest gems and stones from the mines to make a bed for it that would be the most like the Far Mountain.

The dragon, like the Ten Kingdoms now were, was at peace.

'Is it time?' Snow smiled at her, and Lilith leaned forward and kissed her, long and slow, her heart racing as it always did when they were close, and below the people cheered some more.

'Yes, it's time.'

They picked up the large piece of folded silk on the table in front of them and turned to walk away from each other until it was stretched to its full ten feet. She handed her end to Dreamy as Snow handed hers to Feisty, both dwarves dressed in court finery, and then they reunited to stand side by side for the unveiling. Lilith took Snow White's hand and they glanced back and smiled at Grouchy and Petra's grandmother, who'd visited from the Fae Forest for their special day.

BLOOD

It had been a long time – a lifetime – since Lilith had come to this kingdom as an unhappy bride. She'd been a different person then. She and Snow had found each other and everything had changed. It was time for them to mark that change, in a way that would ensure the Ten Kingdoms stayed at peace for as long as possible. It was time to show that strength could come from love.

As she took Snow's hand, and they raised their held hands high to the sky, the dwarves let go, the banner unfurling down the side of the castle. As the image became clear, the crowd gasped and then cheered some more.

Where their sigil had been two roses intertwined, now the roses were wrapped around a golden dragon.

'From now on,' Snow started, before looking at Lilith, who joined in so they spoke in unison, full of love and hope and pride, as the wings beat overhead, 'we shall be known as the Kingdom of the Dragon!'

Epilogue

It was the early hours of the morning and even the moon slept, hidden behind thick clouds, knitting a better blanket of darkness around Aladdin than any invisibility spell. He carefully pulled himself up the rope he'd hooked over the side of the wealthy boat, his slim, small body barely a shadow against the mahogany wood.

'Can you manage or do you need my help *again?*' Bella's blonde hair tumbled over the side as she looked down at him from the deck, the knife in her hand already bloodied. 'We might have forever, but I'm thirsty and I heard the wine collection in this duke's boat is quite extraordinary.'

'I didn't want to interrupt your pleasure.' He pulled

himself up the last few feet, and dropped over the side.

'You know I prefer it when we take our pleasure together,' she whispered in his ear, her tongue flicking into it.

Aladdin smiled and the heart that only beat for her burst into fireworks all over again.

'Then after you, my lady,' he said, drawing his own dagger.

As he followed her down to the carnage that await-ed them in the boat, he realised he'd barely thought of Lilith and Rapunzel and the world outside for months. Maybe longer. Maybe even years. Perhaps they were all dead now. There was one thing he was certain of, however, as he watched his true love draw her knife across a soldier's throat.

They had all lived happily ever after.

Acknowledgements

First, a thank you to all those storytellers of old, Grimm and before, who provided the source material for these stories and without whom all our childhoods would have been a duller place to live.

So much love and thanks go to Gillian Redfearn, editor and friend, who started this journey with me once upon a time, a long time ago, and without whom these stories wouldn't exist.

A massive bow of gratitude to Bethan Morgan for her vision and enthusiasm, and the same to Sam Eades and everyone across the Gollancz and Orion spectrum who has had a hand in bringing these books to life. You are all amazing and I salute you.

Big thanks as ever to my agent and friend Veronique Baxter without whom I'd be a far less stable person.

Credits

Sarah Pinborough and Gollancz would like to thank everyone at Orion who worked on the publication of *Blood*.

Agent
Veronique Baxter

Editorial
Gillian Redfearn
Bethan Morgan
Zakirah Alam

Copy-editor
Tara Loder

Proofreader
Margaret Gray

Editorial Management
Jane Hughes
Charlie Panayiotou
Lucy Bilton
Samantha Jepp Panteli

Audio
Paul Stark
Louise Richardson
Georgina Cutler

Contracts
Dan Herron
Ellie Bowker
Oliver Chacón

Design
Nick Shah
Rachel Lancaster
Deborah Francois
Helen Ewing

Finance
Nick Gibson
Jasdip Nandra
Sue Baker
Tom Costello

Inventory
Jo Jacobs
Dan Stevens

Marketing
Lucy Cameron

Production
Paul Hussey
Katie Horrocks

Publicity
Jenna Petts

Sales
Catherine Worsley
Victoria Laws
Esther Waters
Tolu Ayo-Ajala
Karin Burnik
Anne-Katrine Buch
Frances Doyle
Group Sales teams across
Digital, Field, International and Non-Trade

Operations
Group Sales Operations
team

Rights
Rebecca Folland
Tara Hiatt
Ben Fowler
Alice Cottrell
Ruth Blakemore
Marie Henckel